Overtaken

By the same author

BARCELONA PLATES

THE DOG CATCHER

Alexei Sayle

Overtaken

SCEPTRE

First published in Great Britain in 2003 by Sceptre
A division of Hodder Headline

A Sceptre book

3 5 7 9 10 8 6 4 2

All characters in this publication are fictitious and any resemblance
to real persons, living or dead, is purely coincidental.

A CIP catalogue record for this title is
available from the British Library

ISBN 0 340 76768 5

Typeset by Palimpsest Book Production Limited,
Polmont, Stirlingshire
Printed and bound in Great Britain by Clays Ltd, St Ives plc

Hodder and Stoughton
A division of Hodder Headline
338 Euston Road
London NW1 3BH

ACKNOWLEDGEMENTS

I would like to thank Patrick Devlin very much for spending so much time so eloquently answering my idiot questions on matters of architecture and the building trade and also for introducing me to Michael Scott whose insights into the world of construction were invaluable. Special thanks must go to Jocasta Brownlee at Sceptre and to my editor Rupert Lancaster, my agents Cassie Mayer and Robert Kirby at PFD. And of course, as ever, Linda.

CONTENTS

[illegible] books [illegible]
directions, doubt and [illegible]
impressions [illegible]
[illegible]
and tentative handling [illegible]
[illegible]

'Very nice.' That's what I always used to write in those comments books that they have on a little side table in churches, hotels and restaurants, for you to record your impressions in. 'Very nice.' No matter whether the place was good or more likely bad, I would inscribe it in a weak and tentative hand not wishing to cause any upset. Of course I could say that things then were by and large very nice.

Now I scrawl long, ranting denunciations, using words like 'gallimaufry', 'jackanape', 'poltroon', ink splattering like black blood across the pages or I calligraphy poetical, elliptical, looping encomiums. Sometimes I might do a funny little drawing of a kangaroo, or on other occasions smuggle the comments book away with me under my coat to a quiet place where for a few hours I may compose a sad story; sometimes I simply write 'the pies, the pies'.

I

I remember I said, 'So I'm woken by a phone call at the crack of half four in the afternoon. Do you remember about six months ago I bought a derelict house in Liverpool, a late Georgian townhouse on Upper Parliament Street, then sold it to a young couple, criminal lawyers, on the basis that I got the contract to renovate it to their specification?'

Siggi asked me, 'Is that the beautiful house the council hung on to for thirty years just to keep their old worn-out washing-up bowls in?'

'No,' I replied, 'it's the beautiful house they donated to the fraudulent community arts centre. So anyway the job that I done on that house was meticulous.'

'"Meticulous" – it's your median appellation.'

'Precisely. I'm a complete perfoctionist. For example I fitted sash windows above what their architect required in the main specification, which ended up costing *me* money. Now their spec also happened to call for a particularly rare kind of brushed aluminium combined light switches and dimmers fitted throughout the house, which I did.'

''Cept?'

'Which I did 'cept in a dogleg of a downstairs corridor of the very back of the back of a dark, distant, underground extension at the remotest rear of the house . . . where I fitted one single, plain, white, plastic, standard light switch.'

'It's what you do,' said Siggi. 'Like in Persian carpets, they always weave a deliberate flaw because only God can make things perfect.'

'No, I just ran out of aluminium switches.'

'You twat!' Siggi suddenly shouted.

'What, what is it?' I asked, alarmed.

'Toyota van just cut me up.'

'Oh, okay,' I replied, relieved. 'So anyhoo, it's the bloke from the criminal couple on the phone and he's whining . . .' It sometimes seemed to me that most of the people I sold my homes to were lawyers. Crime and punishment was our industry, when you saw a documentary about prisons on the TV and they interviewed the head of the warden's union in the prison he would often be a scouser and when they interviewed the prisoners they were all scousers too! As if Liverpudlians have boxed off both ends of the lower depths of the criminal justice system. The scousers don't get to inhabit the upper depths though – QCs, barristers and judges, that's reserved for white public schoolboys like my client. I've always thought it odd that all these solicitors and barristers and judges come from this rarified world – private school, university, bowl of nuts on the sideboard, weekend cottage in the Dales, yet they spend all their working days side by side with the absolute used cat litter of society – junkies, pimps, thieves, murderers. I wonder how it affects their view of society, it doesn't seem to give them any profound insights into the human condition that I've noticed, they all appear like dickheads, the ones I've met anyway.

So anyway I'm doing this lawyer's voice for Siggi and I say, '"It's just, you know, the final thing, Kelvin mate," he says. "We love the house, don't get me wrong, mate, you and your guys, your builder guys, mate, did a fantastic job, mate, it's just that that switch, white plastic switch is like the final detail. That white plastic switch is really like, you know, screaming at us, it's spoiling the rest of the basement, well the whole house really, the entire neighbourhood in fact. It's like we've got X-ray vision: even if we're in the attic we feel like we can see it, down there at the back of the house. Honestly Michaela's getting quite down about it; she's spent the last couple of nights in an Executive Double at the Campanile Hotel by the Albert Dock."'

'Oh, get over yourself, tosspot,' Siggi said.

I asked, 'Are you talking to me or the tosser in the Toyota van?'

'I'm talking through you to this lawyer guy.'

'Right. So I says, "Of course, Mr Harris, a thing like that, while it's small it can be an enormous irritant," I says. "Look, give me twenty minutes to shoot round to the wholesalers and pick up the right switch, another fifteen to get to your place and then I'll swap it over quick as you like." The lawyer, he breathes out with this sort of tremble in his voice, "Whoo, thanks, that'd be great, Kelvin," he says. "No problem, Mr Harris," I replies. "I'll be right there."'

'Then what did you do?' asked Siggi.

'Then I put me coat on, I walked outside, I got in me car and I set off for the circus.'

Siggi said, 'It's not a circus it's a circus.'

'Eh?'

'It's spelled cee, eye, arh, capital kay, you, ess, ess. CirKuss, not a circus. Completely different kind of thing. Loyd read about it in a magazine he got free on a train. Not like we used to go to when we was kids: mentally ill lions, sexually suspect birds in high-cut spangly outfits showing their twats, a ringmaster in a top hat with a whip. I mean if that isn't a symbol of patriarchal hegemony I don't know what isn't.'

'No, neither don't I.' There was a sudden bleeping in my car. 'Hang on, I've got call waiting . . .'

It was our friend Loyd. 'Where are ya?' he asked.

'I'm on the M57 'bout half an hour away from the circus,' I said. 'Where are yous?'

'We're there,' he said. 'We're in the council car park, on the seafront, you know, by where the miniature railway runs. They always make me think of the trains that used to run to Dachau those trains, but you know . . . sort of smaller.'

'It'd make a great ride at Legoland.'

'Is Siggi wit ya?' asked Loyd.

'No, she's in her own car, about five minutes behind me.'

'Cool, we'll see ya in thirty then.'

I switched back to Siggi.

'It was Loydy, him and the others, they're there. So what did it say in this article about the circus?'

'Did you say "circus" or "cirKuss"?'

'I said "circus" but from now I'm going to say "cirKuss".'

'Mind that you do. So the article said that the cirKuss was a modern reinterpretation of the old thing in a ring and that they were a collective and that all the performers were drawn entirely from countries where there had been civil war or genocide or regicide or some other extreme kind of "cide".'

'Have you noticed the blue stuff they put the big razor in in the barber's is called "Barbicide"? Is that a mass murder of Barbers? Or possibly Barbies?' I'd been storing this up to tell her for a while. 'Or the mass murder of Barbie dolls?'

'No,' Siggi said firmly, 'they're very hard to kill are Barbie dolls. Every little girl knows that if you're not nice to them it's your Barbies that wake up at night, pick the lock of the toy cupboard and murder you while you sleep.' I found it cute when she talked about when she was a kid.

'Especially that Nazi Barbie doll – Klaus Barbie the Butcher of Lyon,' I said.

'It's a collector's item,' she replied. 'No, they meant that they were from, you know, Afghanistan, Bosnia, Somalia, Rwanda, Zaire, Chechnya. Places where it was a bit difficult to put on a circus right now what with the mass killings and whatnot. Some of them, it said in the magazine, were trained acrobats, jugglers and so on from traditional circus families while others had no acquaintance of performing at all until they had joined the cirKuss. The show they put on is drawn from their collective experiences and one of the few features it has in common with the old, shitty, discredited kind of circus is that they are both in a tent.'

'It makes no sense.'

'What doesn't?'

'The pies, the pies.'

'What the fuck you talking about now, Kelvin?'

'You'll pass it when you hit the slip road,' I said. 'There's this green railway bridge that goes over the slip road on to the A59 and somebody's written on it, like years ago, "The pies, the pies".'

'So what?' she asked.

'So what, it bothers me. I don't know when I first noticed it, it was just suddenly there, "The pies, the pies". It was certainly before I got the TVR, perhaps before I had the Porsche or the Range Rover or the XK 8 or the Maserati 3200 GT, which would make it at least five years ago. Thing is that not only do the words make no kind of sense but that there's also no single other piece of writing on the bridge, even though kids have written on everything else: walls, phone boxes, lamp poles, the odd squirrel that's stood still for too long, yet apart from "The pies, the pies" the bridge remains unsullied.'

'I think you just like saying, "The pies, the pies" all the time.'

'True. So one theory I have is that either the bridge is incredibly dangerous to be on, so perilous that even the thickos who scrawl their tag everywhichwhere think better of it, or the guy that wrote it died and nobody's been brave enough to go up there since, even to get his body. But here's another thing: the maintenance schedule on that bridge must mean it's repainted something like every four years yet "The pies, the pies" is always there. Now either the painters carefully paint round it or as soon as it's covered over somebody reinstalls it.'

'I've just seen it!' she shouted, laughing. 'I've just seen it and I've never noticed it before. Fuck you, Kelvin, I'll never be able to pass it now without seeing it, you fucker.'

'Fucking hell,' I said, 'you're motoring ain't ya?'

Still laughing she said, 'If your clock goes up to 160 mph I always reck that's what the car's manufacturers want you to do.'

'Try telling the cops that.'

There was a pause then she said, 'I've got a theory for you. There's this guy, right? Whose nickname in the drinking dens he inhabits is "The pies, the pies" and he's so fucking hard this guy, I mean he'd have to be to climb on to that crocodile-infested railway bridge with the 250,000 volts running through it and the land-mines that litter the gravel; he's so hard that once he wrote his name up there nobody else has ever dared to cover it up or add to it.'

I said, 'Could be. I sometimes think that I'd get up there and add to it myself, write my name "Kelvin" or something cryptic, maybe like "Make my meringue Mr Attlee". Something like that. I'd almost certainly do it except for the fact that I always forget absolutely and totally about "The pies, the pies" once I've driven past it.'

'Driven past what?' she said.

I said, 'Stop fucking flashing me, will you, I know you're behind me.'

Back then I was the sort of man who didn't take much notice of living things apart from people. Not even most people. I was only really interested, really engaged with my small group of five friends; everybody else seemed fuzzy round the edges. Other than my friends, what I liked and what I could name every species and sub-species of were: cars, buildings, guns, bridges, aeroplanes, clothes, motorcycles and kitchen appliances. What I had no idea about were animals, flowers, trees, shrubs, fish and rock formations.

If I had a contract out in the countryside I would often navigate my way around by the cars that were parked in the villages I went through. When giving directions I'd say to people, 'You turn left at the village that's got the Mitsubishi Shogun parked on the corner by the church, you keep going till you see an old burned-out Bedford CF van then take a left and stop opposite the metallic blue Ford Focus.' Of course if anybody moved their car I was fucked.

So when I pulled up next to Loyd's van in the municipal car park on the seafront at Southport and Siggi slotted her sports car next to my sports car I ignored the radiant, showy, seaside sunset, the ornate floral borders and an extremely rare kind of kestrel and instead I enjoyed looking at the sinister hulking bulk of Loyd's van in the descending darkness. It really was a cool-looking van, probably the only one of its kind in the country. Loyd had bought it during a walking holiday we'd taken in Los Angeles.

There were six of us who were the closest friends there could possibly be. My name's Kelvin. I persist in thinking that I was named after the editor of the *Sun* newspaper, a man called Kelvin McKenzie, who was revered in our house. I persist with this idea even though that can't possibly be right because I was born in 1970 which was long before he was around. I'll tell you what, though, when I was growing up in the late seventies, early eighties, when Liverpool was run by militant socialists, having right-wing parents was a disturbing experience. I remember once we had to hide a Young Conservative in our attic after he'd been chased down the street by bomber-jacketed heavies from Councillor Hatton's 'Static Security Force'.

My mum left us when I was ten so it was just me and my dad after that, plus his occasional girlfriends. He continually went on at me about self-reliance, not being a scrounger, paying your own way in the world and it always made perfect sense to me. In our street there were kids whose parents never seemed to work but always had plenty of money, who sat on the step all day through the summer in their shell suits drinking beer; still their kids got the newest *Star Wars* trooper figures before anybody else and wore those big red Converse baseball boots then threw those out and got the latest Nikes with the weird laces everybody used to put in. I didn't want to be like them.

Not to say we were rich or anything – my dad ran a café near to Liverpool's football ground. It was called the Kop

O'Koffee and we lived above the place, the smell of bacon leaking into my bedroom as I slept. The café made enough money, mostly from match days, for me to be sent at the age of eleven to a private school in Cheshire. The uniform they forced us to wear made me even more conspicuous in a neighbourhood where self-improvement was considered a form of fascism. There's not many kids that got into fights in the street because some other kid calls your dad a 'reactionary class traitor'. It was like living in one of them books written by Chinese women about life during the Cultural Revolution.

So that's me, at the time this story starts. I'd say I was of above average height, dark hair, definitely overweight though not morbidly obese yet. There was my best girl friend Siggi, tall, sharp-featured with a blonde crew cut; Loyd, my best mate – the nerdiest black man you'd ever meet, he had one of those combined palm PC/phones that he wore clipped on the belt of his cargo pants, along with a Maglight torch and a Swiss Army penknife in a pouch. Loyd's wife Sage Pasquale was also a big woman, almost strapping you might say, but very attractive; there was Colin, Jewish, thirty-twoish, gingerish, and finally there was Colin's much younger girlfriend Kate who, surprisingly given his relative ugliness, was a very, very pretty little brunette.

We were very close, all went together to see plays, films, exhibitions at least a couple of times a week, talked all the time on the phone, e-mailed and texted, took at least four holidays a year together. I'd say we'd been pretty much everywhere in the world where you could easily get a drink. Only a couple of years ago Colin had introduced a previously unknown type of cerebral malaria into the north-west of England after a beach holiday we'd taken in Cambodia. As

Colin said, that country was great when we went there but really it's been ruined now. In the last couple of years it has somehow lost its innocence.

So the walking holiday in Los Angeles? Well, about four years ago we all abruptly one day desperately wanted to get into walking. It's funny, you think when you get an idea like that that it's all your own, it's unique to you, you've plucked it out of the air; only when you look back on it a year or two later do you see all the magazines you read at the time included big features on walking boots, Gore-Tex jackets, the fun lives of hill shepherds and how walking is the new thing.

So where were we going to go on our walking holiday? The six of us would go round to each other's houses excitedly clutching the beers and street vendor foods of the country whose brochures we were poring over that week. Still it was hard to decide: would it be exploring the canal towpaths of the Black Forest? Fourteen days rambling the lakesides of the Argentinian pampas? Or three weeks falling off the goat tracks and down the steep crevasses of the High Atlas Mountains? Nothing really appealed to us until Sage Pasquale suddenly said, 'Do you remember that Michael Douglas film *Falling Down*?'

'Yeah.'

'Directed by Joel Schumacher,' said Colin.

'In that film, he abandons his car, Michael Douglas, and he walks right across LA to the sea at Santa Monica.'

'Where Robert Duvall shoots him,' said Colin.

Sage Pasquale ignored that. 'I've always thought it would be amazing to walk down some of those boulevards of LA.'

'But didn't the guy in that film get attacked by gangs and stuff before he was shot by Robert Duvall?' asked Siggi.

'Yeah, I know,' replied Sage Pasquale, with some asperity. 'Like obviously some parts of LA are too dangerous to walk in, we all know that for Christ's sake!'

Yes we did, we knew there were many areas of Los Angeles where no one ever walked; we'd been there before, but when we looked at the maps there still seemed to be huge stretches in the prosperous parts of the west of the city, Hollywood, Westwood, Santa Monica and Beverly Hills in which it must surely be safe to be a pedestrian.

And the thing was, we were entranced with how us it was – quirky, individual, original. We were already thinking of the stories we'd tell other people even before we'd bought the airline tickets to fly there. Thinking back now there were probably little groups of Europeans doing exactly the same thing up and down the boulevards of LA that summer. I fancy now that I saw them off in the distance. Some of them are probably still there, their bleached bones lying in the concrete drainage ditches of the LA River where they had their throats cut.

So in the brown heat of a California summer we trod the sticky streets of LA, along Fairfax Avenue to the Farmers Market we went, down Wilshire Boulevard to the famous La Brea tar pits we shuffled. ('La Brea means "Tar Pits" so they're called the Tar Pit tar pits,' moaned Siggi.) Up 107th Street to the famous Watts Towers we limped.

Yet rather than being the quirky fun we imagined it would be, the whole thing was a horrible, unpleasant experience right from the start. See, it turns out you cannot tell what Los Angeles is like from a map; all those streets, even in the nicest areas that had appeared benign, even on those streets, the sidewalk would suddenly run out and an evil-smelling culvert would cut across our path forcing us to step into six lanes of hurtling traffic, or there would be a new mini mall that had erupted where the map said was sidewalk, with high razor-wired walls that we had to scale if we wanted to get round it to the identical mini mall on the other side.

But we couldn't stop. Every morning when we gathered in the lobby of our hotel Sage Pasquale would hand out complex route maps and photocopies of points of interest and if anybody suggested we had a day off her face would go all closed and tight and we were more frightened of her than we were of the Crips and Bloods and lone maniacs who were waiting out there for us.

One day, our sixth, while we were sheltering from the sun under an overpass of the I-405 on Santa Monica Boulevard and Colin was emptying blood out of his shoe, a Range Rover did a U-turn and stopped next to us; the driver pushed the passenger door open: it was the English actor Ian McShane, his hair painted the same black as the Range Rover. He said, 'I knew you had to be English, nobody else white would be walking here without pushing a shopping cart full of cans. Would you perhaps like a lift to somewhere less terrifying?'

But Sage Pasquale shouted, 'No, we're on our holidays, go away!'

He looked pityingly at the rest of us and he went away.

Later on that day we were walking a particularly alarming stretch of La Cienaga Boulevard: a lowrider crammed to the roof with massive crack-confused Tongans had just crawled past us for the third time when, passing a car lot with rows of triangular plastic flags hanging in the limpid air, Loyd spotted a black V8 Ford Econoliner van with tinted windows, six velour-coated swivelling captains' chairs, folding tables, carpet up the walls, a fridge and electricity sockets, its sinister bulk rising above the Lincolns, Pontiacs and over-bumpered Volkswagens. Loyd gave a cry and said he simply just had to have it right there and then. We all immediately said, 'Oh yes, it's fantastic!' and, 'That's the greatest van I've ever seen!' The salesman in the orange blazer and the polyester trousers with the belt buckle that spelled out 'Handguns' never had an easier sale. From then on we were able to ride the freeways to the beaches and the deserts without it seeming like a bad idea that we had once thought we could walk it.

After the holiday the van was shipped back to Britain on a container ship and Loyd forced the computer games design company he worked for to let him keep it as his company car. Loyd's bosses absolutely hated seeing it there in his named parking place looking like some sort of Syrian taxi – they'd much rather he drove a black Audi TT like they all did; Loyd said it really was rather surprising how conservative nineteen-year-olds could be.

When one of us wasn't present, if you'd heard us talking about them, sometimes you'd have thought we hated each other. 'Him and his wife already buy most of the tickets for most of the shows, choose the restaurants, suggest the holidays,' Colin said. 'Now since he's got that fucking van and he's started driving us everywhere we have to do everything when he wants us to do it.' Colin was always a bit overheated in those days. He had until recently been married to Paula who was thirty-three, exactly the same age as the rest of us. Paula and Colin seemed as happy a couple as Loyd and Sage Pasquale, though admittedly their life was a bit more complicated because they'd given birth to the only child that we'd managed to produce between us, a boy of fourteen whose existence we were barely conscious of. The idea that Colin and Paula were married seemed to be a fact as solid as that Chester was up the M56 or that golf was shit; when they split up I had to go to Chester to check it was still there. Colin had not seemed at all unhappy being married to Paula but then he'd met Kate, a student teacher at a school he'd been inspecting; pretty soon he was also inspecting Kate and had a permanently dazed, distracted air about him. Siggi said the Australians had a phrase for the state Colin was in: they called it 'cunt struck'.

One person bringing in another who was ten years younger, was prettier, sexier than the rest of the gang meant there was now a slight but persistent buzz, like a faulty neon light in what we'd thought was the perfect flawless bubble of our group, but by ignoring it and never speaking of it we managed after a while to stop noticing.

As well, though he was the one who'd wrecked the marriage, Colin was being really difficult with Paula and his kid. I thought at first that Kate might have been a steadying influence on Colin but instead she was behaving even more mental than he was. Say a situation would come up with Colin and his ex-wife where he would be supposed to be picking up his boy for a weekend stay at his new flat. At the last minute he would either not turn up or would suddenly say he had to change the time, then he would get on the phone and scream abuse at Paula, how she was a conniving slut, how she had ruined his life, how she had cooked a particularly unpleasant casserole in 1997, stuff like that. Then Kate would take over the phone and she would scream much more creative and hurtful abuse as told from the woman's viewpoint. Both Colin and Kate told Paula that they couldn't ever reliably say a time when they would be able to see Colin's son because their lives were so busy and important, but they somehow still found the time to sit outside Paula's house in a rented van for half the night, only driving off when Paula ran out and threw a microwave oven through the front windscreen.

Siggi and Sage Pasquale were extremely upset and said the whole thing put them in a very difficult position: at first they tried to continue seeing Paula but that made Colin very unhappy; he worried they were telling her secrets so in the end the two girls started avoiding Paula. Now she was no longer one of the group; the girls said they found it easier that way.

That remark that I mentioned before, Colin's comment about Loyd and us having to do everything when he wants, he made it about a month before we went to see the cirKuss. Colin had booked a prominent table at a brand-new brasserie that had opened in the centre of Preston and said he wanted everybody there because he and Kate had an important announcement to make.

After thirty minutes Loyd and Sage Pasquale still hadn't arrived and then Loyd phones up and says he can't come because they are having problems at work with malfunctioning runaway gypsy inmates on *Auschwitz Kommandant 3* for the Microsoft X box, but as Colin said, 'It's because he didn't book the fucking place himself and he knows we've got something really important to say.'

'So go on say it anyway,' pleaded Siggi.

'Yeah, go on,' I added.

'Well all right,' Colin mumbled sulkily. 'It's just that me and Kate have' – he paused – 'decided to become inspectors for the *Good Food Guide* and this restaurant was to be our first report.'

Kate said, 'We were particularly keen to find out what your thoughts were concerning the "Platter of Pudlets" which we'd heard is a huge serving of tiny authentic Welsh puddings in their individual ramekins presented on a wooden board.'

'Now it's all a fucking mess because Loyd and Sage Pasquale aren't here,' whined Colin.

'No, you mustn't get disheartened,' said Siggi. 'It's people like you two who can do so much to raise the standard of dining out in the north-west.'

I said, 'Yeah, who'd have thought it ten years ago: that these days there are restaurants in the Golden Triangle' – by this I meant the lands bounded by the M62, M6 and M57 – 'as good as any you'd find in Paris, Madrid or Rome.'

'Thanks to dedicated people like you two,' chimed Siggi.

'That's right,' I attested. 'You two.'

Me and my friends, apart from Sage Pasquale, had all been born in the city of Liverpool, but one by one in our twenties we'd migrated to a small Lancashire market town about fourteen miles away. We all had lovely homes that, bought during the low prices of the mid nineties, were completely paid for, giving us plenty of disposable income. With the area's excellent motorway links to the north, south and east we could travel to see all kinds of cultural events that were on in Manchester, Liverpool, Southport, Lancaster, Preston, Bolton. That year alone we'd already been in the audience for the Eels, Eminem, Paul Weller playing an acoustic set at the Empire Theatre, Liverpool; we'd stood in front of new works by Chris Ofili and Tracey Emin at the Lowry, Salford; we'd gone to a poetry slam at the Lancaster Literary Festival; witnessed touring productions of *Les Liaisons Dangeureuses*, *The Nutcracker*, Pina Bausch and her Dance Theatre of Wuppertal; seen comedians and operas; got our cookbooks signed by two TV chefs at Waterstones in Manchester; not to mention that at the age of thirty-three we were still clubbing it in Liverpool and Manchester to top DJs most weekends.

In the municipal car park on the front at Southport Loyd had slid the side door of the Ford back and the other three were sitting around the fold-out table in the dark interior drinking champagne and eating a plate of mini sashimi. 'Hey Kelvin, hey Siggi,' they said and passed two glasses out.

Me and Loyd were best mates from way back; he was a kid that came to live in our street when we were five, the only black family for miles. We'd met when he called my dad a 'reactionary class traitor'.

Colin and Loyd became mates at the comprehensive they went to. Siggi had been Loyd's girlfriend at school for a while; the other women came a bit later, after we'd all left school.

For Colin, school was still very real even though he'd left it fifteen years before: he'd often talk about things that had happened to them there; he'd say to Loyd, 'You remember that time when we was all in the library and . . .'

One time when we were staying in a villa on the island of Lanzarote he was going on like this and I drifted off and started thinking about a thing on the telly I'd seen the previous night on the satellite TV about 'Tomb Raider'. They'd shown a sequence out of *Tomb Raider 2*, the game not the movie. It was some bit where Lara was swinging from rope to rope above a canyon then she dived into a cave and inside the cave was a series of wood-panelled rooms that she had to run through. Steadily through and through those rooms she ran. And the thing was that to me those rooms were so, so familiar, more familiar and real than the room I was in while I was thinking these thoughts, because when I'd been playing that game I'd spent hours and hours, day after day, getting Lara through those rooms and yet they were dreamlike and insubstantial, they were not real and because they were not real I'd forgotten them utterly until I saw them again on the TV and then they seemed realer than anything else. Well, to me school felt like those suddenly remembered rooms on the one occasion when I'd gone back for an adult visit. Come to think of it I recall Lara was being chased through those rooms by giant slobbering dogs with the multiple heads of demons, and school felt a bit like that too.

In the summer darkness Loyd closed up the van and we walked in a group across the car park and through the floral gardens to where on a large gravelled patch of land was pitched a rather small grey tent. Much smaller than I had imagined it would be, much smaller than you could really believe a circus could be performed in. It didn't look like it had been manufactured as a circus tent at all, it looked more like something an army might take on manoeuvres for the generals to have their dinners in.

Behind the tent a strange collection of trucks were ranged in a precise line. As I said before I know my cars and trucks. I was a man who occasionally bought magazines about vans and commercial vehicles to read in the lavatory, and these seemed to be of several different makes that I'd never seen before. The trucks were of the same basic sort, raised high off the ground on two or three axles clad with big chunky black tyres: the phrase that came into my mind was 'border patrol' but I wasn't sure why. The vehicles had all been painted a uniform matt grey with the word 'cirKuss' stencilled on the side in white; most of them had box bodies with small slit windows cut in their sides and steps leading up to stout metal doors. Set slightly apart was another truck that had a large generator on its back and was clattering quietly away to itself; thick black cables led from the generator across the gravel and under the canvas of the tent.

Round the front of the canvas structure a string of lightbulbs ran either side of a tiny avenue of sticky Astroturf that led up to the entrance of the cirKuss tent; the doorway itself was a grinning mouth set in the leering twenty-foot-high face of a demon. On the other side of the demon-head entrance I noticed a sign embellished with a familiar blue and gold logo which read: 'CirKuss acknowledges support from the EU fund for Strategic Vivication and Urbacity, Lancashire Arts Council and the North Western Branches of Mr Tuffy Tune, Exhaust Centres.'

A few other clumps of people, some holding the hands of children, were drifting up the walkway and buying their tickets at a booth set just inside the mouth, like a tooth with a person in it. We didn't have to visit the tooth booth because Loyd had already booked our tickets over the internet at a discount, so we went straight inside.

When our gang went to see anything anywhere the six of us would invariably sit in seats that were ten rows from the front to the left of the entrance; this was compromise seating which had been agreed on after long and sometimes acrimonious debate, because Colin, Kate and Sage Pasquale when left alone were frontsitters, Loyd and Siggi were backsitters and myself, I was a middlesitter. There were a couple of us who had asked why couldn't we sit apart? where we wanted? where we felt comfortable? but Sage Pasquale wouldn't allow this. Anyway the tent was so extraordinarily cramped that there were only five rows of steeply raked seats inside it and we had to cram ourselves into the third row with our knees drawn up like the gargoyles on Notre-Dame Cathederal.

Facing us was the usual circus ring carpeted with sawdust but perhaps a third of the normal size. Looking up into the roof I saw amongst the lights, which were already starting to microwave the audience, a tangle of ropes and swings.

Directly opposite the entrance, across the other side of the ring, there was a proscenium arch about eight feet high and nine feet wide, red velvet curtains drawn across it. Above the arch on to a tiny platform a trio of musicians gingerly edged their way, the wooden scaffolding visibly swaying as they took their places on rickety gilt chairs and began playing mournful music of some Eastern European kind.

With the house lights still undimmed some movement to the side drew my attention to a clown or possibly a 'clOwn' who had quietly slid out from the side of the red velvet curtains and was working his way round the ring; his costume and the state of his make-up implied that he had recently been involved in some sort of explosion. His clothes were charred and blackened and hung in strips off his body, his clown make-up was smeared and smudged across his face. Though staggering when he walked, still the ragged man was gamely trying to keep up a cheery pierrot-like demeanour. What he would do, the clown, was to attract the attention of a member of the audience with furious mad waving then when they were focused on him he would very obviously and slowly throw them an imaginary ball. Being malleable and eager to please as most audiences are, the crowd member would mime catching the ball and then would mime throwing it back to the singed clown with a determined grin on their face.

Sage Pasquale, fearing what was about to happen, hissed at me, 'Kelvin, don't.'

'What?' I said. 'What?'

'Please don't fuck with the clown.'

Loyd said, 'He can't do anything if the clown don't throw him the ball.'

'He'll make him though,' she wailed, 'he'll make him throw him the ball.'

'How could he possibly do that?' said Colin, just as the clown caught my eye and pulled a big enquiring face.

I turned to my friends and shrugged.

'Oh fuck,' whispered Sage Pasquale.

I turned back to face the ring and the clown threw the imaginary ball in my direction. I caught it in a showy fashion but rather than pitching it right back to where the clown expectantly waited, all eager expectation like a puppy, I instead made a big play of studying the ball from every side while the others sniggered around me apart from Sage Pasquale who hissed, 'Just throw it back, Kelvin, just throw it back.'

'Okey-dokey,' I said and with a grunt threw the imaginary ball straight through the entrance and out of the tent.

Right after that, even as the audience's eyes were following the non ball out of the tent, I noticed two things: firstly through the rents in his outfit I saw that the clown's muscles were the hawser-like sinews of a man who could pull and twist and punch things; secondly a faint whimpering drew my gaze to the clown's face. The man was genuinely upset at the loss of his ball, staring about him in undeniable confusion. he looked pleadingly at the audience, then he gazed at where the ball had gone, then he looked at the ground, then finally he looked at me and as he looked at me I got some idea of what it was like to stare down the barrel of a loaded anti-aircraft cannon.

The atmosphere in the tent was starting to sink into the sawdust; even the band who up to that point had been sawing away at some Silesian funeral march clanked to a ragged halt. There was no knowing what might have happened next but in the embarrassed, imploding silence the red velvet curtain below the band suddenly stirred and a girl stepped through.

'Oh,' I remember saying out loud, for she was ever so beautiful. I guessed that she was in her mid twenties with absolute black hair tied back in a ponytail. She wore a white one-piece body suit which ran from long slender neck to pubic bone, she had white skin and black eyes the shape of a cat's, and on her long legs were white tights and on her feet white ballet shoes. If that didn't make enough of an impression, hundreds of glass beads had been sewn to the suit she wore and the powerful stage lights danced off them so that she sparkled and glinted. For a second this girl stood taking in the scene as electromagnetic radiation in the visible spectrum pinged off her, then she called out to the clown in a foreign language and, hearing her voice, he turned to her, a big soppy smile spreading over his countenance. The girl had been holding both hands behind her back; now she brought one arm out and held it aloft, her hand holding the shape of an imaginary ball. The clown eagerly cupped his hands in front of him and, seeing this, the woman drew back her arm and pitched the ball in a clear and powerful arc towards the clown; he leaped high in the air and caught it, provoking a storm of relieved applause to break out from the audience, mixed with many an angry and resentful glare in my direction. The clown, now happy and smiling, capered off tossing his invisible ball, the girl gave an elaborate bow and skipped back behind the curtain, the band began again with a new tune which sounded like the Schizophrenia national anthem, the lights dimmed and the show began.

Like my friends I was no stranger to the modern animal-free circus, and considered that the acts in this one were pretty standard, not up there with Cirque du Soleil or the show at the Millennium Dome with music by Peter Gabriel, but not down there like the performers outside the Pompidou Centre in Paris. Excepting that the one extra element a night at the cirKuss had was the horrible intimacy. The cirKuss performers weren't as close as if they were in a crowded lift, say, but I felt I was really much closer than I had ever wanted to be to anyone performing anything. There was juggling, there was clowning, there was acrobating, the black-eyed girl did some juggling then performed on the trapeze, the wind rumpling the audience's hair as she somersaulted past only centimetres above our upturned goggling heads with a shower of glass beads slowly raining down into our eyes.

So close were we to each other that it was possible to see the extraordinary effort it took to perform each of these tasks: the groans of the strongmen were uttered in our ears as if for us alone, the sweat of the acrobats drifted in a pungent mist on to the skin of the crowd, the smell of the clowns sizzled in our noses and the closeness, the intimacy, the nearness, made it all seem to me completely and utterly pointless. With a start I thought, Where'd that come from? I felt ashamed of myself as if I'd been caught out dreamily contemplating the long legs of a girl in a wheelchair, because it was an unspoken rule of me and my friends that we tried very hard not to dislike things: we had a feeling, one of those dangerous ones that hovers just below the surface of ever being articulated, that once we started not liking things we couldn't know where it would end; better to assume that by and large if somebody had gone to the effort of putting something on, or if they were famous and could fill a big venue then they had something that was worth saying. Yet the thought was there now and I couldn't dislodge it that these performers were going to such effort, such exertion, such rare skill to what end? There didn't seem to be any story that was being told. I looked around, not at the cirKuss folk straining in the centre of the ring but instead at the rest of the audience: were they enjoying it themselves? It was hard to tell. I had been in so many audiences that I knew they can be liars to the performers and to themselves; it was always very hard for them to admit that what they had come to see was a terrible waste of time, so each new routine was greeted with greater applause than the one before, building to an actual standing ovation at the climax of the first half.

Sage Pasquale liked us to stay in our seats during the interval and discuss what we had seen so far but in one of my many acts of petty rebellion against her I always insisted on struggling out, clambering and trampling over people. I pretended to have a mild case of claustrophobia which somehow only seemed to affect me during the intervals of shows.

I told my friends I only stood in the foyer or on the pavement outside but really it was a little secret pleasure of mine to get far away from my mates for a few minutes: to leave the venue entirely and to visit a pub or bar as distant as I could safely run to and still get back in time for the second half. While in the pub or bar I indulged myself in fantasies of aloneness: that I was a mysterious stranger refuelling my mud-streaked Camaro in a dusty Mexican border town or a man with frightened eyes and forged papers changing cross-continental trains at some sinister Balkan rail depot under the obsidian eyes of Kalashnikov-toting paramilitaries. While in reality I was in a hotel cocktail bar in Wigan.

On this occasion as I stepped down out of the banked seating area and into the tiny foyer of the tent, wondering whether I was still fit enough to sprint to the Yates' Wine Lodge on Lord Street in my personal best time of two minutes and eighteen seconds, I saw standing by the entrance to the big mouth the girl from the trapeze, dressed now in a short blue skirt, blue high heels, stockings and a low-cut blue top with a tray strapped to her front on which I could see were arranged tubs of some kind of snack food.

Nobody else was buying as, coldly, she watched me approach. 'Ah, the funny man,' the girl said when I got up to her, speaking in a thick foreign accent. 'You know you really upset Valery, trowing his ball away like dat.'

I was hoping she hadn't noticed I'd been the one who'd messed with her friend's head but I still said defensively, 'Well, it wasn't a real ball.'

'It was to Valery,' she sniffed.

I didn't really want to get into an argument with a woman whose friend was a very strong clown, who had the muscles of a decent middleweight herself and who up close was the most blistering-looking fucking bird I'd ever seen, so I thought it best to put on a contrite voice. 'I know, I'm sorry,' I said. 'I was just showing off to my friends. It's not my fault, it's the group dynamic, honest. For a minute there I thought Valery was going to kill me.'

'Wouldn't be first time,' she said, refusing to bend to my apologetic tone.

I thought a change of subject might come in handy. 'Hmm. What is that, is it food that you're selling?' I said in a stiff voice that suddenly sounded odd to my own ears. Unable to stop myself, I realised what I was doing, taking on her accent. Anybody with a strong inflection could have me talking like them in no time at all. In Chinese restaurants I would often get nasty looks from the waiters because I had suddenly acquired a Chinese accent, though I thought in all fairness that they should appreciate it was not a crude one. I didn't do any of that 'velly solly' stuff but rather spoke in the accent of the indulged only son of wealthy traders from Xi'an Province who had been educated at a Western private school and then had gone on to USC in San Francisco to study mechanical engineering or something like that.

In answer to my question about her tray the girl looked down as if surprised that she was holding it. 'Is Khabapchivi,' she said.

'Dah, I see. Vat is that dat exactly?' I replied.

She thought about it hard, screwing her face up and staring towards the roof of the tent. 'Umm, dar . . . Well . . . is like Gobubchaki but slightly less vortery.'

'Dat's hard to reeseest,' I said, handing over two pounds

for a small polystyrene tub that had a plastic spoon sticking straight up in the food. Smilingly I put a small globule of Khabapchivi into my mouth and chewed. It tasted like Birmingham. 'Hmm . . .' I said. 'There's certainly sometink—' Before I could say anything more the girl interrupted.

'Show starting again. You better get back to your chair, funny man.' Then she darted through a flap in the canvas and was gone, leaving me to dispose of my Khabapchivi in a council rubbish bin. Just as I was going back in to the show I saw a stray dog go up to the bin, sniff it then run off whimpering.

In the second half of cirKuss there was a lot more tumbling, flying through the air and knife throwing, pretty much what would be happening outside in the centre of town by now, I thought. Then the band got out of second gear for the first time that night and clanked into 'Last Train to Clarksville', by the Monkees, for what was obviously meant to be the climax. The girl came on again dressed in an orange boiler suit, carrying three nail guns of the type I knew they used on American building sites. By the girl's side was Valery, also in an orange boilersuit, carrying a huge gas cylinder on his shoulders which he dumped in the centre of the ring, raising a cloud of sawdust.

As the band played he took a packet of different coloured balloons from his pocket, selected one, filled it with gas then twisted it into the shape of a bird. All the while the girl had been juggling with the nail guns; she was amazingly adroit, spinning and catching the unwieldy objects with effortless ease then sending them flying back up into the dome of the tent. As he created each bird Valery tucked it under his arm till he had quite a flock there. Also during all the juggling and the balloon folding the rest of the cast had come on, slithering along the ground clad in skin-tight, multicoloured outfits with their faces painted, possibly to resemble lizards – it was hard to tell.

Now that he had a lot of birds Valery released one into the air and when it got about ten feet high, without missing a beat, the girl shot it down with a nail, causing the lizards to emit a low moan and to writhe about; another bird went up to meet the same fate as the first. Each time the girl nailed a balloon bird the lizards would wriggle around in simulated agony and plead with her to stop her destruction of rubber bird life but she carried on, doing a little dance of rejection while still tossing the nail guns about. I was familiar with those nail guns myself and reckoned the girl had them set on hair trigger, for though I didn't think anybody else noticed quite a few of the nails went flying off into the darkness, and finally I was certain I saw a lizard take one in the thigh, though fair play to the fellow he kept on dancing and didn't flinch for a second. Another reptile pulled the nail out quickly and a dark stain began to spread under his costume.

After the show we left our cars parked where they were and walked down to the dark beach. We were going to eat at a restaurant which was on a boat anchored out in Southport Bay. The restaurant was called the Gravy Boat and it was reached by a World War Two amphibious landing craft which was waiting for us on the sands, its diesel engine chuntering blackly to itself. We climbed a ladder into the open back of the olive-green wheeled boat.

'To me the birds represented hope, which was destroyed by the West's failure to act in Bosnia,' said Kate as the machine sped across the sands and plunged into the black waters of the Irish Sea.

On the way back Colin said, 'My prawns were a bit tough.'

When we got back to the car park it was 1 a.m.; my car in the moonlight looked low and sinister, like some kind of half-glimpsed sea monster. We all said goodbye and the others drove off. I was just about to get into my vehicle when I saw the girl from the cirKuss who was leaning against a sea-rusted balustrade sucking on a cigarette in a continental fashion.

'Nice karr,' she said to me in a friendly manner, the previous frostiness seemingly having melted. 'I not seen before, what is?'

'TVR Cerbera,' I replied, then pointed out to the bay. 'You see that next town up the coast, where the lights are twinkling?'

'Yah.'

'That's Blackpool, that's where they make these TVRs.'

'Blackpool, is that where you come from?'

'No, I'm from Liverpool – that's the other way,' and I pointed. 'East.'

'Oh yah, Orchestral Manoeuvres in the Dark, dey are from Liverpool.'

'Well, Birkenhead actually, but yeah that's close. So where do you come from?' I noticed that for some reason I was talking in my own voice and not imitating her accent.

'Luzhney,' she replied immediately.

'Right,' I said. 'And where would that be exactly?'

'Ermm,' she said, thinking hard, 'is near Lake Lucik, on de eastern side by da big boatyard.'

'Right,' I said again.

Then there was a long pause until she said, 'Maybe one day you take me for drive in your nice karr.'

'Erm, yes, one day yes, maybe I will one day, yes I will maybe,' I said, hurriedly unlocking and wriggling into the driver's seat.

'Well, goodnight,' I called as I closed the door and started up the big clattery straight six.

'Goodnight, funny man,' I heard back through the imperfectly fitting canvas roof.

As soon as the hands-free was connected I told Siggi about it.

She said, 'So you think she was coming on to you?'

'I guess.'

'And you ran away despite the fact that you've seen for certain that she can put both legs behind her head?'

'I know but . . . I just thought a girl like her was too . . .'

'Beautiful? Talented? Exotic?'

'Serious . . . I don't want to get involved with somebody who's seen whatever it is she's seen. You know my motto: a few bob, a few larfs and nobody gets hurt.'

'Maybe you're ready to give serious a try.'

'No, I don't think so, I'd have grown a beard or something if I was.'

'You think there'd be some outward sign?'

'Yes, there'd be some outward sign.' Changing the subject I asked, 'So when are we going out again?'

'Saturday,' she said. 'Frank Skinner at the Manchester Evening News Arena Manchester.'

'Oh yeah.'

'Oh yeah.'

* * *

Saturday was not usually a big out night for us, firstly seeing as that was the night every idiot went out, the 'Bridge and Tunnel' crowd; secondly because nearly every other Saturday in the season Liverpool FC would be playing at home. If Liverpool FC had been playing at Anfield then me, Colin, Loyd and Siggi, who all had season tickets, would certainly have gone to the game. We would have watched the match from our seats, seventeen rows back to the left of the main Kop entrance, then we would have gone on a crawl around all the pubs that were still standing from our school days, then we went to our own homes, had a takeaway and went to bed early.

However this weekend it was an away match. The Saturday before had been the first game of the new Premiership season and the Reds had been up against one of those London teams composed entirely of Frenchmen or Africans who spoke French. The cockney supporters sang:

In your Liverpool slums
In your Liverpool slums
You look in the dustbin for something to eat
You find a dead cat and think it's a treat
In your Liverpool slums
In your Liverpool slums
In your Liverpool slums
Your mum's on the game
and your dad's in the nick
You can't get a job 'cause you're
too fucking thick.

I said to Loyd, 'That year when I was in London I remember once I was standing on a corner in Mayfair or Kensington or somewhere and every stopped car at the traffic lights was a Porsche 911 or a Ferrari, or a Bentley.'

'That's because there's so many rich people down there,' said Loyd.

'Exactly. Here in Liverpool if you've got a smart car it's a rare sight, other people notice you, it means something.'

Loyd said, 'In the country of the blind the GTi'd man is king.'

'Exactly.'

Just then the teams came running on to the pitch. I loved the colours you found at the football match, colours of a purity you never got in real life, the acid-clear reds and blues of the shirts the players wore, the impossible green of the grass on which they ran, the total black and whiteness of the balls they kicked and tossed and bounced off their heads. The only other time I had seen colours of such otherworldly purity was on the tunics of a troop of Horse Guards that had suddenly come riding out of the dawn mist in a street in St John's Wood when I was down in London for that year.

Then after that for ninety minutes plus a fifteen-minute break I had no independent thoughts at all, for I became part of that huge animal which is the crowd. As if falling into sleep I let myself sink into the mass so that my individual thoughts and movements were only one component in the bulk of a gigantic beast. I was freed from the responsibility of conscious thought; I believed what the crowd believed: that the penalty against us was unjust no matter how clear the foul was, that the forward was onside no matter how great the gap was between him and the opposing defenders, that the other supporters were a pack of lying cockney cunts and their players were a bunch of untalented, shiftless, cheats until the day when they came to play for Liverpool FC when they were somehow transformed into the best players in the world.

2

The original plan for the trip to see Frank Skinner at the Manchester Evening News Arena had been for me to go with the others in the van; if I'd gone in the van I would have been able to have me a few drinks. Though in general I liked to drive myself in my own car to things, I did think that seeing a comedian was miles better if you'd got a few drinks inside you. The alcohol gave you more courage to shout stuff out, which definitely made the whole show go better for everyone present. I knew for absolute certain that comedians really loved it when they had somebody like me in the audience, someone who talked back to them and yelled out witty comments and took the piss out of their appearance and shouted out the punchlines to their jokes a split second before they said them.

Unfortunately, though, I couldn't go in the van because in the afternoon about two hours before I was due to meet the others I'd got a phone call telling me that someone I knew had just been taken in to the Royal Liverpool Hospital and I had to go and visit them. This man had been waiting a year and a half for me to restore a single piece of lead flashing that had fallen off his roof and he had finally tried to replace it himself. The man had inevitably slipped and fallen off the roof, breaking his arm plus his femur in three places and suffering severe concussion.

When I got to his hospital bed the man was full of

apologies. 'I'm sorry, Kelvin,' he said. 'What was I thinking of? I know you were going to do it, I just thought . . .'

'Honestly, Dad,' I said, 'you've got to start trusting me. I was actually going to do your roof today. I've actually got the piece of lead flashing in the boot of the car, I was actually, literally on my way round to your place when the hospital phoned.'

'I know, I know, please forgive me, son, please, I'm so sorry.' Then he started crying.

So what with stopping off at the wholesalers in Liverpool to pick up a strip of lead flashing, time was moving on. It would be impossible for me to get home, park the car, change and make our rendezvous so I had to phone Loyd and tell them to set off without me, I'd try and catch them up on the M62 so we could drive into Manchester together.

As soon as I topped the flyover in my TVR at the Rocket pub where the motorway starts, even though it was a late summer evening, the sky suddenly went black with stormclouds and a few seconds later rain began to fall. Big heavy drops that quickly formed puddles and then when the drops landed in the puddles each made a little bubble, a perfect glassy dome as it hit.

Again I phoned Loyd. The first thing my friend did after he got behind the big steering wheel of the Ford was to slip a bulky microphone headset affair on to his head, he then plugged this into his phone which in turn he clipped into a bracket protruding from the dashboard. Loyd had even bought a woodgrain cover for his Nokia which matched the fake wood veneer inserts on the van's dashboard, so he needed to take off the shiny metal façade which his phone normally had and replace it with the woodgrain one. After all that he was ready to start driving, about five minutes after he'd first got behind the wheel. Like I said, he was the nerdiest black man you could ever meet.

'Where are ya?' I asked Loyd.

'We're just turning off the '57 on to the '62.'

'Not too far then. I should be able to catch ya if I put me foot down though this rain's a bit of a pig. What's the traffic like where you are?'

'Solid but moving.'

'Fair enough,' I said. 'Put me on speakerphone and let me give a big shout out to everyone.'

Loyd switched me over and the gang all shouted, 'Hi! Hi, Kelvin! See ya soon, Kelvin!' I heard all their different voices. Every one of them.

I shouted back, 'Hi, gang!' and then rang off.

Slowly I pressed the big drilled aluminium accelerator pedal and turned the windscreen wipers to their most rapid setting, adding the sound of their flack-flacking to that of the rain zizzing off the canvas roof and the wail of the big straight six as the sodium lights clicked by on the M62.

Round about junction 10, with the humps of the big old bomber hangars at Burtonwood like whales in a grey sea, I came up behind the Ford van. My friends were travelling in the outside lane, my TVR was about three car lengths back on the inside when we hit the flashing orange lights, the big yellow boards and the 50 mph warnings blinking on the overhead matrix signs which told drivers that we were about to be switched into a contraflow system. Everybody dropped back from 80/85 mph to the 60 mph tradition agrees you do when the signs say 50.

A few seconds later row on row of cones, and arrows

made up of hundreds of flashing bright orange bulbs, led us across into the westbound path from which we had been separated seconds before by concrete reinforced armoured steel barriers; these had now been replaced only by a tranche of plastic magicians' hats. By this time I had leapfrogged the two cars in front of me and was off the nearside of the van: I could see Colin and Siggi in the rear seats leaning forward to join in with what the others were saying. After perhaps half a mile the flow both east and west was swapped back to the left-hand bore of the M62 by more signs and another sinuous ribbon of cones, which came immediately after we passed under a bridge whose cover for a second eerily stopped the sound of the rain drumming on the taut roof of the TVR.

Indeed this silence seemed to last much longer than it really could have done, for, as the snake of cars entered the curve, I saw a big four-axle tipper, one of the Japanese ones that had never really caught on in Britain, coming towards us at a speed well over the 50 limit, spray flaming out from its sides. The driver, realising he was never going to make the sharp turn to his left, tried to brake instead, forcing all the weight from the full load he was carrying on to his leading wheels. One tyre failed to take the sudden weight and exploded. I saw it go, a colourless explosion followed by ribbons of black rubber springing up into the air like joke snakes bursting from a can bought at a magic shop. All grip now gone and down to the spark-showering metal rims on its leading wheels, the tipper slewed out of its own lane, detonating through the cones, popping them aside like skittles and he hit Loyd's van square in the side. The brute power of the truck was such that it took the van right across in front of me, the powerful headlamps of the tipper lighting up the inside of the Ford showing all my friends sitting calmly in their seats. Then I was past them and the motorway was as it always was, cars and cars and cars all the way to the North Sea a hundred miles away to the east.

Except that looking in my rear-view mirror I could see there was nobody behind me. I was the last one to come through, the two eastbound lanes of the contraflow were empty and on the opposite side the traffic was beginning to bunch to a halt, brake lights and hazards blinking on and off in the streaming rain. Because of the roadworks the hard shoulder was being used as one of the lanes but as there was no other traffic it didn't matter when I stamped on the brakes and slithered to a stop in the middle of the carriageway. I dialled 999 on my mobile phone and it was only then, when connected to the emergency operator, that sound seemed to return, both inside and out, with a cacophonous rush. Speaking to the woman operator, a decade of watching police and hospital dramas on TV gave me the convincing jargon. Calmly I said, 'There's been a collision eastbound on the M62 approximately a mile east of junction 10. Tipper truck versus van, multiple casualties, I repeat multiple casualties and risk of fire.'

The operator, picking up on my tone, told me units were being despatched and would soon be on scene, then she broke the connection.

Clambering out of the TVR I fell to my knees for some reason, I didn't know why. Remaining on all fours with stinging palms for a few seconds, I then got to my feet and stood for a little while longer on the tarmac swaying backwards and forwards; collecting myself, I began to run up the M62.

* * *

The tipper truck had been crammed to the top and above with a load of rubble, bricks and broken cement, making it tremendously heavy and giving it enough terminal velocity to drive Loyd's van into the concrete side of the bridge at 70 miles an hour. After pushing the van against the wall the truck had then mounted it, ridden up over it, crushed it downwards, compacted it, before coming to a stop rearing up into the air resting its weight on the torn cadaver of the van.

All around on the motorway drivers from the stalled traffic were getting out of their cars and staring intently at the wreck, as if attempting to prise apart the ragged scraps of metal and glass, the battering oily girders, the rocks and stones, solely by the use of mind control.

A rescue party began to form, a camouflage-panted man pulled a fire extinguisher from his winch and aerial-adorned Land-Rover then ran over to the crash and squirted foam on to some wisps of smoke curling from under the wreckage. An elderly man wearing a tweed jacket and a dicky bow climbed out of a big BMW 7 series, said to the crowd gathering around the smash that he was a surgeon, don't try and move anybody, clear the rubble, has somebody called the paramedics? Good, don't try and move anybody, wait till the paramedics get here, I'm a surgeon. Then clambered to the back of the van and stuck his head through the hole where the rear window had been and started talking to somebody in there. A woman from an old Ford Fiesta said she was a nurse and inserted herself in the hole next to the surgeon. I sort of wondered why everybody was stating their jobs. I wondered if I should say, 'I'm a builder.' Then stick myself into a hole. I supposed I could of course mention that they were my friends in there under the metal, but it seemed like that would be pulling rank, grandstanding sort of, drawing attention to myself in an egotistical way and I didn't want to do that.

So instead I walked around the other side of the truck and climbed up the slippery grass bank to where the tipper's cab was hanging in the air. Another group of motorists, perhaps those who preferred a happy ending, were talking to the truck driver through the open hanging door of his cab. He seemed to be conscious and if not able to talk was at least able to swear.

'Fuck, oh fuck,' he said, 'fuck, oh fuck, my fucking leg. Fuck, oh fuck.'

'You'll be all right, mate,' said one of the drivers, 'the paramedics are on their way.'

'Fuck, oh fuck,' said the truck driver by way of reply.

In the distance I heard the first wailing of sirens cleaving the sodden air.

The first unit to arrive was a Lancashire Brigade fire engine coming the wrong way up the eastbound carriageway, then a St Helens ambulance, a Merseyside Police Range Rover, two more ambulances and another Lancashire fire engine. Soon there were enough flashing lights for a disco and a load of confident bossy men and women in reflective jackets ordering each other about. The second fire crew and a pair of paramedics, dragging a big square bag like they were planning a picnic, came clambering up the bank to attend to the truck driver. Clearly useless, I went back down the steep grass slope to hover near the wreck of the Ford van.

That's when I noticed that there was a strange groaning sound coming from the top pocket of my shirt: what must have happened was that because Loyd's was the last number I'd dialled on my mobile, at some point I had accidentally pressed the redial button and was now connected to my friend inside the mangled van.

I put the phone to my ear. 'Hello, mate?' I said.

'All right, mate,' I heard Loyd reply. An energetic enough reply though there was a wet, quavering quality to his voice that for a second made me feel dizzy. In the background, over the phone, I could hear the little man who'd said he was a surgeon murmuring to someone.

'How you feeling?' I asked.

'A bit flat,' Loyd said. Then he laughed, 'Hee, hee, hee.'

'How's everybody else?' I enquired. 'How's everybody else?' I repeated, but Loyd seemed to not be listening any more and just kept going 'hee, hee, hee'. In strange stereo I could now hear the fire brigade's saws beginning to cut into the metal of the van both over his phone and a microsecond later floating towards me across the roadside grass.

I felt totally useless amongst all the competing emergency services going about their proficient work but then a thought came to me that as long as I didn't hang up my phone I could somehow keep Loyd alive, like one of those machines that they hook you up to in the hospital that do the breathing for you, a life support kind of thing. Glad to be doing something, I checked the battery level on my Nokia: it was two-thirds full, good, plus signal strength was excellent out there in the open flat countryside so I reckoned it would easily be possible to keep Loyd breathing until the fire brigade managed to cut him out of the smash and got him and the others to the nearest hospital.

Now that I was a vital part of the rescue effort I felt able to get closer to the wreck of the Ford van. By now the fire crew had most of the side of the vehicle hacked away; briefly I looked inside; I thought it was like one of those motorised advertising hoardings that you get at busy road junctions where three different adverts are cut into strips and pasted on to triangular rollers the shape of Toblerone bars that pivot from one picture to another, except sometimes the rollers get stuck, the motor jams or something, so that one poster is mixed with another; say one advert is for a van and one is of some models in swimsuits and one is for some jagged strips of metal maybe, so they're all jumbled up with strips of the people and strips of the van and strips of the jagged metal arms and wheel and head and hand and seat and gearstick.

Slightly behind the straining fire crew and the bright green overalled paramedics there was a big traffic cop, a sergeant judging by the stripes on his uniform. He was holding a bright spotlight over his head so that the firemen and the paramedics could see what they were doing.

I went over to this man also holding up my mobile phone in imitation of the way the policeman was holding the spotlight. I said to the policeman, 'It's all right, mate, I've got Loyd, he's the driver, the driver, the driver of that van there, I've got him . . . he's here on my mobi . . . it's all right see? As long as I keep him connected, it's sort of like a life support thing, you know what I mean? As long as I don't hang up, right? It'll be okay. Look, I've got battery power for hours yet so there's no problem there and signal strength is excell—'

The sergeant looked at me. 'Do you know these people?' he asked, indicating the insides of the van with a nod of his head.

'Yeah, they're my mates, I was behind, I saw it all happen.'

The sergeant called to another policeman. He said, 'Max, take this . . .' and he handed the lamp over to a younger constable, then he took me by the arm and led me a little way off from the grinding sounds and the flashing lights.

'I'm sorry, son,' he said, then again, 'I'm sorry, son, but they're all dead.'

3

There'd been so much for me to do in the first few days after the accident that a maniacal buzzing energy kept me going. I felt like the promoter of some sort of wildly out-of-control event, like a rock festival set in an inaccessible location where the leading acts had cancelled and only a fifth of the tickets had been sold. All the organising of the aftermath seemed to flow through me. As the main witness there were endless statements that I had to give to policemen who hadn't spoken to the other policemen that I'd already done my act for. There were unending relatives who had to be sat with, comforted, tranquillised, disarmed while on their way to the truck driver's hospital ward, multifarious and amazingly diverse undertakers who had to be dealt with, death certificates that had to be got, wills that had to be read and most of all funerals that had to be gone to.

Unfortunately it seemed that at some point in the twentieth century the art of holding a funeral, like the art of cooking and the art of tasteful interior decoration, was something that had deserted the ordinary people of Britain, from whose ranks the families of my five dead friends came. So that the funerals of Colin, Kate, Loyd, Sage Pasquale and Siggi were terrible mish-mashes of poetry reading, favourite tune playing, rambling reminiscing in front of congregations only a few of whom had dressed soberly. Only the most restrained were attired in what they considered to be appropriate funeral garb, i.e. black leather bomber jacket, white shirt, black tie, dark trainers.

I don't think I would have got through it without my dad; he checked himself out of the hospital and, encased in plaster as he was, was more use than all the ineffectual vicars I met over those terrible days. His main contribution was to put me in touch with an older generation of female relatives who still knew a little about how to hold a funeral and who possessed special pickle dishes that were to be used only at wakes.

Nevertheless I think because I was doing so much and because the services were so shitty anyway, I failed to gain any of the catharsis that proper funerals are supposed to provide and instead a few days after the last of them all the activity stopped and I drove off a cliff of depression.

First there was a sort of stunned non-feeling. I had never realised you could feel so much of nothing, so much nothing that the world outside me virtually ceased to exist; everything beyond the inside of my head appeared to be covered in a light haze, like smoke drifting across the motorway on an autumn morning. I felt utterly unanchored, unattached to a universe that existed without grief. Often I wondered idly why my body didn't float up into the air, so unconnected did I feel to the real world.

All the separate orderly days that had been chopped up into such neat portions of time, the slices of life once firm and filled with phone calls, appointments, assignations, e-mails, text messages, conversations, plays, cirKusses, concerts, became rotten and runny and fluid so that night no longer followed day in orderly sequence but instead became random. Sometimes a row of short mornings, nothing too difficult to get through, were followed by a night that seemed to last for one hundred and seventy-two hours, a night filled with screaming and weeping and the jabber of the things that are screened on TV in the middle of an unendable night.

If I'd ever momentarily considered it I guess I'd thought that depression was pretty much like being very very sad. Now it was here it was nothing at all like that: instead there is a horrid, metallic, chemical quality, a level of internal pain that made life endless and very hard to get through.

Yet to my surprise I didn't go completely insane, though I think that might have been a relief. Every day waiting apprehensively for full-blown madness to arrive, like a man expecting the last train home that he knows is packed full of football hooligans. Is this it? I'd think to myself every time a memory of my friends convulsed me in a knot of misery. Is this it? Is this the thought that does me in? But when the train came the hooligans pushed me about a bit, scared me, made me pee myself with fear then more or less left me alone.

The single significant date in all my relentless future was the one set for the trial of the tipper truck driver. His name, I found out, was Sidney Maxton-Brown, a self-employed haulier and the owner of a small fleet of trucks; he was fifty-four years old, which made him the same age as Siggi's dad. When the Lancashire traffic police crash investigators examined the vehicle he'd been driving they found that over half the tyres had a lot less than the required amount of tread on them, the truck was carrying almost twice the legal load of an amount of toxic waste for which there was no documentation – they still didn't know where it was from or exactly what it was – record checks revealed that the man had never taken a test to be a heavy goods vehicle driver and a doctor's report said one of his eyes didn't work very well because of a pronounced squint.

On that basis he was vehemently pleading not guilty to manslaughter. Especially in times of stress I'd always had a bit of a thing for authority figures. I remember the college I went to in London backed on to a fire station and I'd often hang around when the firemen were playing volleyball hoping their ball would come over our wall so I could throw it back and talk to them. This time my uniformed substitute mum was the police families liaison officer, a kindly detective sergeant of about my own age. I suppose it was his job to be nice to me but still it seemed like it was also in his nature. He said, referring to Sidney Maxton-Brown, 'Kelvin, the man really doesn't get it, he genuinely thinks he's done nothing wrong. I've watched the interview tapes; he keeps saying he was only trying to make a living for his wife and for his daughter Susam. He seems to think that the fact that he never signed on the dole allows him to kill people. He says that he always provided, when his family needed food or medicine or a tattoo or a new ringtone for their mobile phone.'

Over the months between the accident and the trial I paid almost no attention to my building business which you'd think would screw it up, so it surprised me and everybody else that my firm was doing better than ever. I went out with a girl once who'd been on that Prozac drug for a while: she said the main side effect was that the quality of her tennis game improved immensely; she reckoned this was because the numbing effect of the drug meant she didn't give a damn whether she won or she lost. It was sort of the same with me: my almost complete inattention to my firm resulted in its ever increasing prosperity.

Over the years I had become as much a developer as a builder and if you were medium-sized like me you had to be innovative in your thinking, that's how you stayed ahead: I'd been one of the first to notice that city centre office blocks from the 1960s didn't have the ducting space in the floors and ceilings for the amount of cabling and air-conditioning the modern workplace requires, but that their narrow profiles were ideal for converting into stylish flats. I'd also got in on the ground floor of the mental hospital boom, as early as 1994, redeveloping a small former secure psychotics unit in Wigan as twenty-eight luxury duplex apartments. Lovely flats they were, only marred slightly for the inhabitants by the risk of them waking up with one of the former occupants in the bedroom wondering where their locked ward had gone. I'd converted churches, factories, deconsecrated pubs; now, after the crash, I absentmindedly bought properties – houses, schools, warehouses – and would by accident sell them, to a bloke I couldn't remember meeting, for a massive profit: I acquired some land in payment of a debt and the next day the site was chosen as the location for the UK headquarters of a major television home shopping network.

As a result of my vagueness all my subbies – the chippies, sparks, plumbers – had to take greater responsibility; it was no good asking me for a decision about anything, I just stood there humming. I guess they liked me or felt sorry for me or something because they responded with amazing flexibility, showing initiative and conscientiousness, so that all my contracts were finished on time, on budget and to a very high standard, which was an almost unheard-of occurrence in the building game. I suppose if major business leaders want their corporations to do well they should consider offing their five best friends.

In the lobby of the Crown Court in Liverpool on the first day of the trial I kept looking around in confusion at the dwarfish, stunted creatures who swarmed about me, their baseball-capped heads about a foot below mine, smoke chuffing out of their mouths as if they were miniature trains at the seaside and I would think, Who *are* these people? Then I would recall where I was with a jolt and I would say to myself, Oh, yes, they're *criminals*.

Inside the hot wood-panelled courtroom itself I sat with the relatives of the dead. Across the other side of the public gallery it was easy to spot members of the extended Maxton-Brown family, seeing as each of the male Maxton-Browns had inherited the family squint, so they sat waiting for the show to begin with their eyes shooting off all over the place like fireworks. Occasionally the accused's family would dart angry stares at the relatives as if it were their offspring who were on trial for deliberately and recklessly driving themselves into the path of an innocent tipper truck. At one point I noticed a crop-headed fifteen-year-old Maxton-Brown girl making stabbing and throat-cutting motions at Sage Pasquale's seventy-five-year-old granny.

Inside the court there was that air of a show about to begin. I wondered if there was a backstage like at the theatre; perhaps the judge was at that moment peeping through a curtain, asking the clerk of the court, 'What are they like today?'

Except it never did begin, the show. I'd experienced

similar decompression a couple of times before: once I remember when the Prodigy had failed to turn up for a concert at the City Hall in Leeds and once during a play in Liverpool when an actress kept forgetting her lines. First there was the same impatient murmuring and muttering from the audience, then you could see the backstage staff self-consciously having whispered consultations with each other, then finally there came the announcement: 'Ladies and gentlemen, unfortunately Keith Flint says he simply can't be fucked coming up here so . . .'; 'Ladies and gentlemen, as you can see one of our cast has been having problems so I am afraid tonight's performance is cancelled. If you wish . . .'

Back in the well of the court I suddenly noticed that Sidney Maxton-Brown's barrister was the lawyer whom I'd sold the house in Upper Parliament Street to, the one who'd been bugging me about the brushed aluminium light switch. I'd gone round and fitted the correct light switch a week and a half after the accident; I think he was a bit surprised to see me there on his doorstep at 4 a.m. with a screwdriver in my hand continually breaking down and sobbing while I fitted it but I think he was pleased.

Since the accident I'd completed all those sort of tasks that I'd previously been avoiding. The day-to-day lies and evasions of the builder were poison to me now; I found it hard to stand lies any more in any context and again, though it wasn't my intention, this trustworthiness did my business nothing but good. I had discovered I was no longer able to be dishonest in any way. Now, reflecting on it much later, I think in the back of my mind, which was as crowded with guilty thoughts as the smoky backroom of an old-fashioned pub, there was the vague feeling that one of the reasons the crash had happened was because of my former dishonesty.

The clerk of the court was passed a folded note, he stood and announced to us all: 'The trial of the Queen versus Sidney Maxton-Brown is suspended and will resume at two this afternoon.'

In a hubbub of mystery we swarmed and fought our way out of the trying room. The relatives collared the Merseyside Police families liaison officer outside in the shabby corridor. Standing at the back of the group, I heard him say to their frantic questioning, 'What's happened is his solicitors have finally persuaded him to plead guilty to "Causing Death by Reckless Driving".'

'What does that mean?' asked Siggi's dad.

'He'll be sentenced this afternoon.'

'What'll he get?' asked Colin's brother.

'Ten years I imagine will be the sentence,' said the policeman.

'Yeah, but what does that mean in reality? He won't be out for . . . ?'

'At least five, could be more,' he replied.

All the relatives started shouting:

'It's not enough!'

'He should be there for fucking life!'

'You fuck off, he's done nothing! He's being persecuted is what it is. We're going to launch an appeal, then we'll get compo like all them paddies.' This came from a fat-legged Maxton-Brown woman.

'I don't think you can have an appeal if you've pleaded guilty,' said the police family liaison officer.

'You can fuck off too, you Jew pouf!' she shouted.

I was so lonely I said to the policeman, 'Do you fancy going for a drink?' I didn't want to lose him but I suppose his job was done now and his training told him he needed to disengage to maintain his boundaries.

'Oh, thanks, Kelvin,' he said warmly like he really wanted to do it, 'but I got to get going, get home. They're digging up the Dock Road and it's added about thirty minutes to my journey. Fucking bastards, every time I go past there's no sod working on it.'

'I know, it's bonkers,' I replied, tutting sympathetically. 'I mean what's going on with that?'

'I've no idea,' he said.

But I did.

Perhaps a month after the accident, having just managed to drag myself back to work, wearing odd shoes and an unwashed pullover with stains all down it – an office conversion it was on the edge of St Helens city centre – still in a terrible state, hardly able to stand for misery, an awful fear was following me around. Something completely ordinary like the sound of wind in the trees could pitch me into such an appalling terror that I shook until my legs gave way and I had to clutch on to a road sign for support.

That day the building's enormous new air-conditioning unit was being lifted inside the structure by a mobile crane. As I stood there, simply watching and getting in the way (my highly competent site agent handled everything so there was no good reason for me to be there, it was just loneliness), I suddenly had the sense that there was something missing. Not able to figure out what it was, I looked all about me before it dawned that the absence was inside rather than out: while in no way could I say it had gone, my awful anxiety had lessened to a considerable degree.

I surveyed the site to find out why this was. In order to make space for the crane to do its work we'd blocked off the road with barriers and traffic was being routed around the site via narrow side streets causing complete chaos; cars and vans were stacked up in all directions, unmoving as far as could be seen. Oddly I realised it was this chaos that was making me calm: all the drivers and passengers in the cars were safe as long as they were stuck in this traffic jam I'd created. It was me who was making them safe; as long as my crane kept them stuck here nobody could possibly run into them and kill them. I was saving their lives.

What had made me fearful of everything over the past months was the terrifying truth that you had absolutely no control: my friends had been killed and there wasn't a single tiny thing I could have done about it. I was helpless like we all are. Yet here in St Helens my roadblock was making people safe, I was keeping them from killing themselves in their cars.

Pretty soon the one interference I would make in my smoothly flowing business was to suggest to my people using mobile cranes where there really was no need for them. Since this was virtually my sole input they were happy to humour me. After a while this wasn't enough; next I began getting my sites expanded into the roads they bordered, on various unlikely pretexts so that they blocked off or narrowed major arteries all over the north-west of England. And the thing I learned was *they let you do it*, the councils, the police and the highway agencies; if you told them you wanted to block off the roads, they said okay, take all the time you want, do what you have to do. After the first few times wondering if I'd get caught out, the realisation dawned that I was able to barricade the streets at will. We would put in an application to place a crane at some vital road junction, my men would put up the barriers, then they'd go, the driver would park the crane then he too would go. For a few days I'd leave it there screwing everything up, then the crane driver would come and take his sixteen-wheeled behemoth away again and nobody would know that it had lifted nothing at all.

After that, becoming bolder, I started digging the roads themselves up. See, they all assumed, the authorities that is, that if you wanted to spend money digging up the highway then you must have a good reason to do it. It was inconceivable to them that somebody would part with cash for any other reason. So I would send my men out (usually I got official permission though sometimes I didn't even bother with that), they'd take their jackhammers and their picks, my men, and they'd smash up the fucking killing tarmac, put a fence round it then leave it for a day or a week or a month or a year, before coming back and filling it in so badly that it was absolutely impossible to drive over at any speed. Thousands more lives saved.

That hole in the Dock Road, the one that was holding up the copper – that was one of mine, now coming up for its six-month birthday. And, do you know, it really didn't cost that much at all.

The year I spent in London (Loyd once told me Colin had said I talked about it as if I'd had twenty years before the mast on the Valparaiso run) had been my first year at a famous central London art school.

I'd always been crap at exams. Admittedly the private school in Cheshire that my dad sent me to wasn't what you'd call academic, none of the kids were particularly posh, just had parents who wanted their kids to grow up being hard-working and honest, who thought suing the council over imaginary back injuries was not a viable career path. Come to think of it, I guess not all the parents wanted their kids to grow up exactly honest since a sizeable minority of the pupils were the sons of the big Liverpool crime families, the Gorcis, the Mukes, the Pooles. Still, they weren't going to need any A levels with what they'd be doing.

I guess my work must have been okay because they took me. In 1988 at the age of eighteen going down to the capital I'd been full of happy confidence, assuming I would start making good friendships that would last a lifetime within the week, make that two tops. Back home in Liverpool I'd always been one of the popular kids. I was the funny one, sure, but not a kid you fucked with, okay at sport and able to look after myself. Looking back I suppose a lot of what went wrong was plain bad luck but at the time the world seemed to have turned suddenly and unexpectedly malevolent: firstly the hall of residence where the college put me was one that was shared with a load of different schools and universities in central London. I never met anybody from my own college there, it seemed to be entirely full of homesick Africans weeping in the laundry room. Liverpool humour didn't work at all – my Thunderbirds impression just frightened them.

Still, not to worry, I thought, knowing for certain that I would make friends once college started. I'd always had no trouble making friends, I was the popular guy.

Except that my uneasiness about being away from home seemed to infect everything around me. Normally you would expect each day in an unfamiliar situation that things would become less unfamiliar. I mean that's like a law of science or something, but for me every day of college was still accompanied by the same disturbed strangeness as I'd experienced on my very first hour there. Nothing about the place seemed to stick in my memory: the college building was as impenetrable a labyrinth on my last day as on my first. The cleaners began to suspect some strange voyeuristic motives when they found me for the fourth time crouching in their stores cupboard waiting for an art history tutorial to begin. I often couldn't even recollect where the place was and would catch the tube to some district where I was fairly certain it was situated, then wander the streets looking for it.

On the odd occasion when I did find my way to the college and then found the studio space where I was supposed to be doing my work, things were no better. Painfully I'd manage to get going on a painting, scratching a few reticent marks each day until at least there were some tentative beginnings on the canvas, then a visiting lecturer would come along, he'd look at my painting for a second or two and then say to me, 'No no no, that's complete fetid rubbish, it's weak weak weak, derivative and weak. Anyway, carry on, I'll be back again in nine months.' I mean my art teacher back at school had been really encouraging, telling me how good I was and inviting me round to his house to look at art books and listen to records, but here the staff seemed to regard their primary role as being to stop you painting. I told one of the weeping Africans that I was starting to suspect the staff weren't interested in students unless you were a pretty girl they could shag or your work was exactly like theirs but not as good.

And then if that wasn't bad enough there was the city of London itself. That Underground they've got down there, the map's supposed to be dead clear, isn't it? A miracle of graphic design, they say, but I never got the hang of it the whole time I was there. Sometimes I'd catch a train on a yellow-coloured line, change three times on to routes of various hues, then walk for miles along smelly tiled corridors only to emerge above ground and see the station I'd started off from about a hundred yards up the road. On other occasions I would get on the tube in the middle of London, travel for perhaps only a stop or two, then it would halt and all the power would glimmer off. I'd look around and see I was alone in the carriage, so get off to find I was at a country halt with a white picket fence, hanging baskets of geraniums and big zinc milk churns stacked on the platform. I never even attempted to take a bus.

Then there were my fellow students at the art school who were as impenetrable to me as the tube network. They were either incredibly posh or, if one of the few working-class kids, then they were crude unconvincing stereotypes, like English characters played by American actors in a US sit-com. I recall I did get to a few art history seminars: there would be about twenty-five of us sitting in a circle in an airtight room. I remember this one time the tutorial was about Van Gogh and the lecturer showed us a slide of a painting and he said how you had to see it in a gallery because you couldn't conceive of the richness of the colours from a reproduction and a girl I'd been thinking of maybe talking to one day sitting next to me said, 'You don't have to go to a gallery. Oh, I know that painting; it's hanging in the entrance hall in our flat in Rome. Yes, it really is lovely, the colours really are . . .' And I just thought, Fucking hell, these people have a Van Gogh, and it's not even in the living room it's in the fucking hall! That girl is never, ever, ever, going to want to talk to me, never mind be my friend or fuck me in her entire life . . .

The only person I knew in a city of ten million people was a sort of cousin of mine, who lived not in Lewisham but near it in a place that didn't seem to have a name, who was not exactly an accountant but something near it. This place where he lived, to get there you had to take an overground train smelling like a wet dog from a big railway station then walk for miles through grey roads where the streetlights seemed to hose colour out of the night.

I used to get on the train to visit without checking whether my sort of cousin was in, because if he wasn't in at least another empty evening had passed. On one blank winter Tuesday I travelled over there to find no reply to my ringing on the bell (though the idea had begun to form that the not cousin had started hiding when he suspected it might be me at the door). Turning around, head drawn in, I shambled back towards the station. When I'd got off the overground train I'd bought and eaten four Yorkie bars at a newsagent's in the adjacent parade of shops, but on my return there was only a Chinese takeaway open. I ordered a sweet and sour pork and sat on a plastic chair to wait for it to be ready.

When it came and I peeled back the cardboard lid of the foil container I realised I'd made a mistake. In Liverpool your Chinese food comes on a bed of chips or rice with a plastic fork for you to eat it with but in London it was all the pork stuff with no chips and no fork so that I was trying to eat this orange goo with my fingers, while standing in the street.

With a shudder I threw the food into the gutter and got on a train that was going to Victoria Station. I got off, walked round to the coach station where I bought a ticket on the overnight bus back to Liverpool and was in my dad's house asleep in my old bed by 8 a.m. and in the pub that afternoon with Loyd and Colin.

In the saloon bar of the pub Colin said to me, 'We couldn't believe it when you said you were going to study in London. What the fuck did you want to go down to that shithole for?'

'I don't know now,' I replied.

'I'm not even going to move out of me mum and dad's house for five years,' said Loyd.

'You didn't say anything,' I whined.

'Kelvin, we thought you had a plan,' said Loyd.

'No plan,' I said.

'Let's face it, you're no Siggi,' said Colin.

'No Siggi,' I said.

The year before, when we'd all been seventeen, Siggi had gone for an audition without telling anyone and then got a place at the Bristol Old Vic Drama School. We had a party to see her off and said we'd all visit but somehow didn't, especially not me who was stuck in London. So the first time we saw her after her first term was in the pub at Christmas time. The only thing we noticed that seemed different was she had come back from drama school with a long 'A' so that she would say 'barth' where before she'd said 'bath' like the rest of us. This we all ignored; the only other thing they seemed to have taught her in Bristol was how to fall over. Every half-hour or so she'd punch herself in the chest and drop to the fag-end-strewn floor, then jump up again, but we pretty much ignored that too and after that a chasm seemed to grow between us until she stopped coming back for the holidays and stayed in Bristol.

Occasionally we got reports from her family that she was doing really well down there but families always say that.

Even if she'd come back I wouldn't have wanted to see her. I thought myself a failure at eighteen like some not quite good enough teenage footballer. Considering my future was over, I miserably took a job as a labourer at my uncle's building firm. And there on the building sites I found everything I'd been expecting art school to be. In a pasteurised, safe world I found the sites to be the last refuge of the true individualist: the wild characters I met on the building made my fellow art students seem as distinctive from each other as sausages. I hadn't known, behind those hoardings, how fucking clever and funny and kind everybody was. Everywhere I worked I encountered inarticulate men who could hardly write but whose thoughts were in such a profound form of 3D that they could solve the most complex problems without resorting to any kind of drawing or plan.

Then there is the work itself: think about it, what we builders do is nothing less than we reshape your world. Where you are now, where you are right now this minute, reading this, stop. Look around you – a builder made it. Wonderful men conspired to put it together: labourers you dismiss as thickos built it; guys you step over in the street now they're old and fucked up solved all the problems you didn't know were there; a developer you consider as only one step up from a maggot conceived of it, fought to get permission for it, destroyed rare archaeological artefacts, covered up dangerous chemical spoil to get it constructed on time. Now doesn't that seem as profound as making cakky marks on squares of canvas?

And what's more the money is fucking fantastic. At first

I was a general labourer. Those outside the building think the labourer is the lowest rank on the sites but it's much more complex than that; the other trades, sparks, chippies, plumbers, come and go when their task is completed but the labourer is there right throughout the job from beginning to end so if he wants to, the labourer, he starts to take responsibility for things when the foreman isn't around, deliveries, minor problems, that sort of thing. Then if he's clever he starts to see the opportunities: with my wages I bought a derelict house in the South End of Liverpool, did it up and sold it, made a tiny profit. The next one I split into flats using guys I'd met on other jobs to do the work. The return I made on that place gave me a profile with the bank, which meant they were happy to lend me some money. That money meant that the buildings I bought could be bigger, the risks greater, the profit larger.

Even before I'd gone to London I had learned to drive in my dad's old 1973 Vanden Plas Princess 1300 and could soon afford my own car, a black Volkswagen Golf GTi I bought at a bankruptcy auction.

Colin said to me, 'Kelvin mate, you should think yourself lucky you didn't get a higher education. I mean studying for an English degree has put me off fucking books for life, but you, because you're self-taught you love reading, man, you devour it all voraciously – classical literature, detective fiction, biographies, comic books, modern feminist writing – you don't shove stuff in artificial boxes, you don't worry whether its 'good' or not, you're just wide open to new ideas, man.' Patronising bastard.

One weekend in what I guess must have been towards the end of her third year, on a Saturday morning when I was supposed to be doing some repairs for an orphanage near Manchester, I instead stayed on the motorway and drove my black car to Bristol, having got Siggi's address from Paula, with whom she still fitfully corresponded.

When I rang at the door of the grey terraced house which Siggi shared with two other girls from the drama school, it was answered by a pretty little redhead, still in her dressing-gown though it was the afternoon. She seemed recently to have been crying.

'Hi,' I said. 'I was wondering if Siggi was in.'

'She's at a tap class,' snuffled the girl. 'She'll be back in half an hour, wanna come in and wait?'

'Sure, I guess.'

The girl showed me into the living room, which I noticed with a silent internal shudder was the usual student landfill site; in this case it was made even more untidy by the fact that there were pictures of movie stars torn from magazines and books strewn all over the floor and all over the ratty broken-down furniture. As soon as she got back in the room the girl started crying again. It struck me that there was already a gap between me and this girl, even though if she was in the same year as Siggi she must be more or less the same age as me. I felt like I was an adult and she was a child, albeit one with spectacular tits visible inside that dressing-gown. I stood there enjoying the feeling of being like a grown-up in my narrow dark blue trousers and my cream jumper bought from the Emporio Armani shop that had just opened in Manchester, spinning my car keys round my finger.

The girl continued to sniffle miserably as she made me a horrible cup of instant coffee.

'Erm, is there something the matter?' I finally felt forced to enquire.

In response the girl stuck both her thumbs up at me, which seemed an oddly positive gesture for somebody who was sobbing wretchedly.

She quavered, 'Do you see anything wrong with these?'

'Your thumbs?'

'Yes.'

'No, they seem fine to me.'

'Exactly, that's what I thought. Well, we had a film workshop at college yesterday with Szigismond Wajeckej; he was the cameraman on *The Laughter of Larks*. Did you see it?'

'Not yet,' I said.

'Well, anyway, he took one look at my thumbs and he said they were too broad for me ever to be a success in films. So I've been looking through all these pictures of movie stars and I can't see any difference between their thumbs and mine. Do you want to have a look?' she said, holding out a giant magnifying glass.

'Er, sure.'

For the next twenty minutes I studied the thumbs of the highest grossing film stars of 1991: Clint Eastwood, Harrison Ford, Meryl Streep, Chevy Chase. I could see no difference between their thumbs and those of the redhead. I told her this and she calmed down a little. As she said, 'It's not as if you can get plastic surgery on your thumbs. Not even in Ecuador. I've asked their embassy and they said definitely not. Honestly, the fucking criticism you have to put up with if you're an actress; how are we supposed to live with stuff like that?'

Surprising myself, I found I could see her point, not entirely sure if it was simply because I wanted to fuck her or not but I felt I could understand how horrible and intimate and wounding such criticism must be. Where I worked, in the building game, if you were displeased with someone you might sometimes come up behind them with a length of pipe and smack them with it but there was nothing personal about your actions, it was simply one of a range of options that were open to everyone. But to have a go at a girl's thumbs, now that did seem way too cruel.

Siggi came back from her dance class a little later looking sweaty and dishevelled. At first there was some awkwardness between us about what my motives were for being there, so we were forced to energetically send out signals to each other like ironclad battleships cutting through the grey sea on manoeuvres off Jutland Sound until we had sorted out what I was doing there. 'I j-u-s-t c-a-m-e f-o-r a v-i-s-i-t i-n m-y c-o-o-l c-a-r, I'm n-o-t a-f-t-e-r a s-h-a-g o-f-f y-o-u h-o-n-e-s-t. T-h-o-u-g-h I m-a-y b-o-i-n-k y-o-u-r l-i-t-t-l-e f-r-i-e-n-d,' the semaphore flags flapped.

The Aldis lamp clacked back: 'S-h-e's a r-a-n-d-y s-l-a-p-p-e-r y-o-u c-a-n h-a-v-e h-e-r.'

'Wow, Kelvin,' said Siggi, standing back and taking in my new clothes. 'You look like a drug dealer.'

That night I drove Siggi, the redhead and another girl from the drama school to a studenty-type pub. They told me excitedly that they had put together their own comedy group called the Hitler Sisters and that night they were putting on their own one-hour show in a room above the pub. Their show was called *Am Misbehavin.*

The redhead said, 'Those stiffs who teach us at the Old

Vic School think our dream is a lifetime of playing Titania or Cordelia in the theatre.'

'If we're lucky!' said the other one.

'Or third prostitute with weeping head wound in *Casualty*.'

'Do you know we've spent the last two weeks making puppets out of fag packets?'

'I mean what is that all about?'

'They should be teaching us stand-up comedy not bloody fencing.'

'There's all these great comedy clubs opening now.'

'And there's all these great women comedians coming along.'

'Nelly Shank, Beth Coil, Jenny LeBute, Mrs Patel—'

'I think she's a man.'

'Still, it's not a boy's game any more.'

'No way!'

'Yes way!'

'Party on, dude!'

The upstairs room of the pub where once earnest mechanics had studied *The Communist Manifesto* had now become the Giggle Room. Seated at small round tables, the audience were students and the young clerks who spent their days in the insurance offices around the city and needed an easy laugh when they went out for the night. I thought of all the great laughs we had on the sites and felt sorry for them; I didn't have to pay for it.

I stood at the back leaning against the sweating wall. The lights dimmed and on to the spotlit stage came the three drama students. The third girl sat at a war-ravaged upright piano and while she played all three sang a song about Tampax and periods. Then the redhead did a routine about periods and boyfriends and Tampax, then Siggi sang a song about cakes and periods, then they performed a sketch about a boyfriend buying Tampax for his girlfriend who was having PMT because it was nearly her period, then there was another sketch about what a wimp your boyfriend is when he has a cold, then there was another song about Mrs Thatcher having her period, then Siggi read a poem about 'The Disappeared' of the fascist junta in Argentina, then they finished with a song and dance routine about Tampax.

Throughout the show I experienced a rising sense of discomfort. Not because I was disconcerted by the stuff they were doing: I wasn't entirely sure whether it was funny or not but I'd laughed along with everybody else. No, what had caused me increasing trouble was Siggi.

From the moment she had stepped on to the shabby stage I had not been able to take my eyes off her. I'd always thought that phrase was just an expression that didn't mean anything, like stuff people said about ravens in pies and plucking motes out of the eyes of Pharisees or whatever, but for me and for the rest of the audience it was a literal truth, we could look only at her. The entire crowd were joined in an unspoken conspiracy and the only ones who weren't in on it were the other two girls on the stage. Indeed if anything the other two got more laughs than Siggi did and received more applause because we, the audience, felt awfully sorry for them, so they must have thought that they were doing better than she was and treated her with a certain patronising hauteur.

As the applause died down, after they'd left the stage, I said to the young guy in the overcoat tied with string who was promoting the show and who had been standing right at the back twitching as promoters have always done throughout history, 'Mate, can you tell Siggi—'

'Which one's she again?' he interrupted.

'The one with the talent.'

'Oh yeah, her.'

'Right, well, can you tell her I can't stay like I thought I could and I'm sorry I've got to get back home because I've completely forgotten an important meeting I've got early tomorrow morning.' Then I left.

Driving north along the empty motorways, I thought of how crystal clear this day had been, how every detail sparkled and glinted and was fixed in my memory for ever. If I'd had to, I knew that in six years' time I would be able to tell some detectives which shelf the parmesan cheese had been on in the student girl's fridge, how many buttons were missing from Siggi's blue coat and what the soup of the day was in a café two doors down from the pub where the comedy show had been. A few years later Sage Pasquale won a competition in the *Manchester Evening News* for tickets to a special advance screening of Kenneth Branagh's *Frankenstein*; the little redhead had a small part in it playing a crone and funnily enough up there on the big screen her thumbs did seem to be too broad.

Just like me, Siggi didn't finish her college course but in Siggi's case it was a sign of success not failure. All the shows at drama school she'd been in during the preceding eighteen months, there'd been an agent or a casting director in the audience looking her over. She told me later they were usually middle-aged women who travelled in twos, the agent and a sidekick. They'd take her out for coffee or a drink afterwards, adeptly shaking off the other drama school girls who tried desperately to tag along.

Siggi listened calmly to the plans they laid out for her, the exciting opportunities in theatre and TV that awaited, but it was only when Laurence Djaboff came that she got excited. Laurence Djaboff, founder of the famous Laurence Djaboff theatre group, for whom she willingly abandoned her graduation show. He offered her the leading role opposite him in his new piece, *Hard Wee Man*, the play he'd written about his childhood in Aberdeen's notorious South East End, as the son of the only Orthodox rabbi in the Highlands.

Suddenly interested in her again, the whole gang, apart from me, booked to see the play on its opening night when it came to Liverpool's Everyman Theatre. Apart from the odd phone call and a few brief meetings none of the others had seen much of Siggi in the last three years. They all said they were very excited that they knew someone who was starring in a play.

'Hi, it's Siggi, do you wanna meet for a drink?'

I was extremely surprised to get a call from her on my brand-new carphone. 'Er . . . sure. Welcome back to Liverpool by the way,' I said.

'Yeah, right, come to the rehearsal rooms. Oh, and bring a sports bag with, like, running stuff in it, trainers and shorts.'

'Why, are we going for a run?'

'No,' she said like I was daft.

I got to the dance studio where the Laurence Djaboff Company were rehearsing *Hard Wee Man* half an hour early and watched through a glass panel set in the wall as they soundlessly went through their play like underwater performing fish. Even through a plate of greasy glass the raw power of Laurence Djaboff burned like the heat off a pizza oven. At that time he was at his peak, thirty-five years old, a good ten years more than the majority of his troupe apart from one old bloke who must have been in his seventies. Laurence was a compact bundle of windmilling energy dressed in a sharp-looking Hugo Boss suit, cream silk shirt and highly polished American Florsheim Oxfords.

Right on one o'clock the action stopped and the actors and actresses began to file out of the studio. I edged past them, smiling in a vague way and went inside; only Siggi and Laurence Djaboff remained.

I'd had thirty minutes to adjust to the change in her appearance. In later life people would come and go in my life and would mutate while outside my gaze, but since I saw my friends more or less every day we were changing in ways that were imperceptible to each of us. Siggi was the first person I was close to who had dropped out of my sight for a lengthy period. I was shocked by the fact that she was the same but different: it was sort of like watching *Terminator 2* – the cast were more or less the same as the original film but older, glossier and with more muscles.

'Let me introduce you to Laurence,' she said. While me and Siggi had been been saying hello to each other the great actor had been changing out of the Hugo Boss suit which was his character's costume and into his own clothes. Out of the corner of my eye I'd watched as he'd put on baggy harem pants in striped moiré silk, blue suede pixie boots, a blue linen collarless peasant blouse over which he put a brown leather Sam Browne belt with a suede purse where an army officer would have worn his revolver; on top of all this he wrapped a brown mohair cloak and on his head he put a black woollen astrakhan hat which he arranged in one of the floor-length mirrors at a precise tilted angle.

'Laurence, this is my friend Kelvin.'

'Hi,' said Laurence Djaboff. 'Is this the guy you're going for a run with?'

'That's right.'

He turned to me. 'I've told her I want her to go for a run to prepare for the show tonight. I've sent two of the others to a cemetery, Miles [the seventy-year-old] has got to have sex with a sailor and my female co-star I've sent to the bus station to dance for money. I myself am off to see if I can get into a fight at the airport.'

'That shouldn't be too difficult,' I said.

'Would you like a fight?' said the actor suddenly, in a reasonable, friendly manner. 'Would you like to go to the airport with me to have a fight? I'll pay for the taxi.'

I said, 'That's very kind of you but no, I have to go for a run with Siggi.'

'Are you sure?'

'Yes, pretty sure.'

'Yes, of course. Well, please yourself.' And with a flick of his cloak he left.

As we slipped into the Victorian pub across from the theatre Siggi said, 'Mad cunt that he is.'

We sat in one of the side rooms, afternoon light ricocheting off the bevelled glass as I went to get us both drinks. When I returned and sat down she said, 'I can't remember it.'

I said, 'What?'

'The play, I can't remember my lines in the play.'

'But haven't you've been touring all over the country, performing night after night?'

'Yeah . . . well, mostly,' she said. 'Well, always. I do remember my lines but I'm becoming terrified that at some point I won't, that I'll be standing there one night not knowing what to say.'

'But why would that happen? I bet you're really good at remembering your lines. You're really talented.'

'See, yeah,' she said, becoming nervously animated, 'that's the problem, how talented I am.'

'How can you being talented be a problem?' I asked.

'I'm supposed to be so fucking great, aren't I? There's been all these women casting directors coming down with their witchy wizened little sidekicks saying I'm going to do this or I'm going to be that, but then I started thinking that, well, okay, but it's basic to be able to remember your lines or stand up or not be sick on the stage and if I couldn't do any of those things then I was no better than the crappest actress.'

'But why should you be sick on stage or forget your lines?'

'I don't know, but what if I did?'

'That's crazy; it's like worrying if you're going to be gored by a bull on stage or if your shoes will catch fire.'

Sweat burst on to her forehead and her eyes grew big. 'Has that happened?' she squeaked.

Siggi had five more double gin and tonics before going back to the Everyman. I suggested drinking so much might not be a good idea before performing a play but she said in that case I didn't know anything about the theatre. After lunch, feeling really quite drunk myself, I rang Loyd and asked if it was too late to get a ticket for the play that night.

'I thought you said you didn't wanna see the play?' Loyd said suspiciously.

'I don't remember saying that,' I replied. 'I just thought I'd be busy at a meeting but as it turns out I'm free to see Siggi in her play.'

On the opening night of *Hard Wee Man* in her home town, Siggi, with the whole gang watching, didn't exactly forget her lines, instead she made up some different ones. I can't remember any of what she said now but it was great dialogue, real poetry, majestic, fluid, vivid, and her performance was one of luminous, twitchy energy; the audience's eyes followed her about as if she were a tennis ball: it's just that none of the others in the cast knew what to say in reply.

After the interval Laurence Djaboff came on stage and said, 'Ladies and gentlemen, as you can see one of our cast has been having problems so I am afraid tonight's performance is cancelled. If you wish . . .'

He told us if we applied to the box office the audience could get their money back. So we found ourselves on the street two hours earlier than expected; it wasn't even dark yet. Sage Pasquale and Paula went round to the stage door to find out if Siggi was okay but they were told an ambulance had already taken her to a hospital.

A few months later when Siggi came out of the mental home she took a place on a training course that taught you how to be a further education lecturer; this lasted for a year and then straight out of that college she got a job in the burgeoning field of media studies at one of the many educational institutions that seemed to be opening up in our little Lancashire town and again she became one of the gang as if she'd never been away.

Siggi had once told me that there was an actors Equity

rule that if there were more actors on the stage than there were people in the audience then they didn't have to do the play, they could go home, the show didn't have to perform. Well here, I thought, there was one actor still yabbering and flapping and gimping about on the empty stage but there was absolutely nobody in the audience. Yet the show seemed to be grinding on regardless, though what the point now was I couldn't say.

4

The only possessions belonging to Loyd, Colin and Siggi which their relatives fought violently over were their season tickets to Liverpool FC. I had not felt like going to a match since the crash but this was the last game of the season and I thought I might as well use my own season ticket one last time. It would be terribly painful, almost beyond bearing, that I would no longer be sitting amongst my friends and I'd readied myself for that, but when I got to my own seat, which I naturally expected to be empty, I found an old man I didn't know sitting in it.

'Oohr you?' I said.

'Oohr you?' replied the pugnacious little old man angrily, stretching up his sinewy bantam neck.

'You're in my seat,' I said.

'Fuck off. This is my seat,' retorted the old man. Looking around in confusion, right then Sage Pasquale's sister's husband came down the concrete steps with a hamburger in his hand: when he saw the two of us facing off a faint look of embarrassment crossed his face.

'Oh hi, Kelvin,' Sage Pasquale's sister's husband said and took me in an awkward hug without putting his burger down. Releasing me he continued, 'Ah, oh, we, ah, didn't know you was coming today, we, erm . . . this is Oswald,' he said, indicating the little old man who still sat bristling in my seat. 'We been letting Oswald sit in your seat 'cos he's been supporting the Reds for fifty years, you know, but his seat is right up the back, you know and you wasn't around to . . .'

'That's right, fifty years,' said Oswald. 'Billy Liddle . . . Ronny Yeats and "the Saint" . . . Shankly's boot room.'

I leaned forward. 'Well, that's great, Oswald,' I said, 'but I'd like my seat back now.'

'Ian Rush, Kenny Dalglish, Hysel Stadium, Hillsborough,' said Oswald, showing no sign of moving.

'Look, I don't have time for this. Just fuck off up the back, you scrawny old cunt,' I heard someone say in a voice full of genuine menace. Looking around I realised it was me who'd spoken.

'There was no call for that,' said Sage Pasquale's sister's husband's best mate who'd arrived just as Oswald was angrily shuffling off up to the back of the stand muttering under his breath about the '86 cup final. 'He's been coming here for fifty years.'

At first, still shaken at my sudden eruption, his words didn't go in. I remembered that once, a long time ago, I had had quite a temper but over the years Sage Pasquale's fear of confrontation had meant it had been gradually suppressed, but now I thought, with a familiar clenching of the guts, Sage Pasquale wasn't around so it didn't matter any more. At that thought I abruptly felt like my head was full of popping corn.

Turning to Sage Pasquale's sister's husband's best mate I said simply, 'And you shut it too,' in a way that made the man go white. Then I stared hard at the battered, muddy, end-of-season pitch.

As the game began, squeezed uneasily between Colin's cousin, Sage Pasquale's sister's husband and Sage Pasquale's sister's husband's best mate, I felt confused; I hadn't expected to sense the old joy, of course that would be ridiculous, but I was still surprised by the extreme feeling of contempt that swept over me, not for the players – they just seemed silly, jumping and running and falling over – no, it was the crowd who made me feel sick with disdain. Around me the fans seemed to cycle rapidly through a range of emotions, all of them entirely fake; one second they would be engulfed in operatic ecstasy over some shot sailing wide of the goal and the very next they would be vomiting rage at an opposition player they'd taken a dislike to. Actually, I thought as the mob howled with relish as one of their defenders prematurely ended the career of a promising opposing youngster, it's only the ecstasy that seems false, the rage appears to be real enough. That I should want to submerge myself into these awful people seemed completely ridiculous. I was reminded of footage I'd seen of Hindu pilgrims submerging themselves in sacred rivers bobbing with sacred corpses, sacred raw sewage and sacred containers of nuclear waste.

Abruptly I got up from my seat, edged my way past all the fans too engrossed in the game to pay me any attention; eventually I got to the concrete steps, slowly climbing them till I reached the dark exit where I stopped and turned to take one last look at the muddy grass where the little men ran and jumped. As I wheeled to descend into the cool gloom of the interior I saw Oswald rise from his seat against the very back wall and crouch low on the steps like a spider. The old man's eyes stared hard into mine, and as I began to descend towards the turnstiled my final image was of Oswald scuttling down the steps towards my vacated seat. Stumbling towards the grey river and the electric rail line that would take me home, the roaring of the crowd pursued me like a mugger whispering vile threats in my ear.

Since the accident, I'd not been able to bring myself to drive a car but the town in Lancashire where I lived was connected to Liverpool by the Mersey Link electric railway. The station we had always used to get to Anfield, amusingly called Sandhills, was in a district of refineries, large areas of rubble, car dealerships and abandoned warehouses that ran down to the river.

Above it on a plateau were the red-brick terraced houses amongst which Liverpool's football ground squatted. In a couple more years it was rumoured the club would be moving to a new stadium hacked out of a Victorian park a few hundred metres away.

My route to the railway line took me, first of all, past my dad's old café, my former home now a Chinese chippy, then through a few streets of terraced homes that ran along the edge of the plateau balanced above the steep drop to the distant river. All these dwellings in a grid pattern of six streets were empty and neatly sealed up with perforated steel grilles. The Trotskyist town council which had run Liverpool in the 1980s had bought them all up with plans to build a museum of revolutionary feminism but my Dad said the councillors had spent all the money on trips to Cuba and smart suits instead so the houses had stood empty for over twenty years. From the silent streets I could see clear across to the bilingual hills of North Wales.

A sudden terrible fatigue seized me, memories of all the times I had passed through these streets with my friends and I sank to my knees in weariness and misery.

* * *

There it was in those streets that I found my Thebes. The Greek hero Cadmus searching for his sister Europa in desperation consulted the oracle at Delphi. The oracle ordered Cadmus to drive a cow across the age-old lands into the province of Boeotia. Cadmus should mercilessly impel the poor beast forward, never allowing it to rest for a second, and at the spot where the creature finally collapsed from exhaustion there he should found his mighty city of Thebes. I don't know what that had to do with finding his sister but I suppose you had to do what the oracle said if it bothered to speak to you. Anyway I was both Cadmus and my own cow.

Slumped against a wall, I began to idly speculate on how little these houses would cost to buy from the desperate cash-famished council; the whole network of streets could be mine for the price of a couple of Porsches but then I thought, Where would the profit be? Terraced streets all over the north could be had for nothing because people with money didn't want to live in terraced streets. The ordinary ones dreamed of E-fit houses in the suburbs and the out-of-the-ordinary ones wanted lofts. Sure, everybody was looking for the new loft, but lofts offered big open minimalist spaces, not the front parlours, kitchens, sculleries and back boxrooms of these tight little terraces. More importantly, the big converted warehouses with their solid entrances promised security from the wolves that roamed outside. I'd always imagined it was impossible to make a street secure: suddenly I thought, Is it?

Now I was not one of the big national companies in the developing game but I was doing better than okay. For a start, all the pointless digging up and the crane parking that I was doing meant that my firm's logo was all over the place; this in turn meant everybody in the construction industry imagined I was making a fantastic profit, thus advantageous projects came to me first and I never had a problem financing them since the bank rang me more or less daily offering to give me your money to do what the fuck I wanted with it. I'd always had an edge when finding development sites: the way I did it was partly by having a small regiment of runners, estate agents, commercial agents, people like that, who were constantly on the lookout for properties for me to develop; they got a 2 per cent fee if the deal went ahead. Besides which I bribed a couple of local government workers in the council's Valuers Department with cars and holidays, women and drugs to let me know about the many fine buildings the council had forgotten they owned; it also helped that my stooges were able to fix the price at which the council sold these buildings to me.

Yet nobody had told me about these streets: they didn't think even I'd be interested in terraces. No one was interested in terraces.

But why not? Seeing as you would be able to buy the network of streets entire it would be possible, I calculated, to wall off certain access points topped with historically correct spikes and on others you could install gates, perhaps modelled on those of famous Princes Park, all of it surveyed by CCTV cameras and rapid-response rentabizzies always on call. Then I thought, Seeing as they would be so cheap, why restrict each buyer to one house? Why not take, say, three houses and knock them into one big space, like where the Beatles lived in the film *Help!*. At the ends of several of the streets were empty shops and on the corner of one I could see there was a huge four-storey abandoned pub. I got unsteadily to my feet and hobbled towards it. It was a marvel, built in the Gothic revival style with etched glass windows for the four separate bars on the ground floor, above that large rooms for billiards, meetings and perhaps a restaurant, the third floor was staff quarters and above them attic rooms and cupolaed towers that must give fantastic views south to Wales and west into Liverpool Bay. With the new football stadium being built, I thought excitedly, there would be plenty of wealthy buyers, fans from outside the area, who, rather than endure Liverpool's appalling hotels with their surly staff and shabby surroundings, would be eager to buy a luxury apartment in a secure neighbourhood with its own restaurant housed in a refurbished pub and if they didn't want to eat out maybe the restaurant would deliver. The development could have its own delis and clothes shops, all of it within walking distance of the football ground. Maybe I could sell timeshares there, who knew?

My head full of thoughts, I left the silent streets and walked to the railway station. At first on the rocking train I had four seats to myself but a few stops further down the line a thin blonde woman in a beige raincoat boarded and without seeming to look came and sat on the seats facing me, her knees interlocked with mine, and said in a flat, dull voice, ''Ee keeps punching me in the stomach, so of course I lost deh baby. Mind you it was probably for the best because it wasn't 'is . . .'

I wasn't surprised by this, since about a week after the accident complete strangers, without any sort of encouragement, had begun coming up to me and telling me the most awful, sad stories from their terrible lives. I supposed that there must have been something in my manner which provoked them or perhaps I gave off some hormone, some distillation of misery which alerted other desperate souls to a particular sufferer in their midst. This did not mean these people considerately chose to leave me alone in my pain; instead they decided to add to it by recounting their own desperate tales.

The woman continued – I'd learned not to interrupt them by now – '. . . the kid's dad was this man at work whose wife has motor neurone disease and he's been suffering from clinical depression, so I felt sorry . . . a bit sorry for him and I suppose it showed because then I think he put something in my drink at the firm's Christmas par . . .'

Enduring thirty-five minutes of this, rain had begun to fall and I was in farming country. The town I lived in was where the line terminated. The station was on the edge of the old town centre, down a steep cobbled lane ranged with railway workers' stone cottages.

Along with the Saturday evening crowds returning from the big city shops I toiled up the rain-polished lane; at the top I was forced to stop and rest for a while; memories were again pummelling me: over the road was where somebody had said this, in the park we'd all taken that. I was compelled by misery to lean against the wall of the Station Hotel, a steadfastly rough pub at the top of the lane. My vision would often go out of focus on these occasions; when clarity returned my eyes were looking at a bright little poster in the window of the pub. Looking closer, as figures performed a shadow play of drunkenness beyond the frosted glass, I saw that the poster was advertising a new show from cirKuss, apparently called *Clamdango!*. The poster told me that they would be performing for a week, starting that night and that their cirKuss tent was pitched on a patch of common land located on the edge of town where such things as fairs, circuses and transient homosexual encounters were traditionally held. For some minutes I stared hard at the poster and then slowly walked home.

My route took me along the main shopping street where there were a surprising number of butchers, bakers and greengrocers still surviving. At this hour the shop assistants were folding up their trestle tables, putting the sausages in the freezer and bringing in the fibreglass, lifesize Jolly Butcher figures as I passed.

Going out of the centre walking along a busy road lined with sandstone Victorian villas; cars and trucks swishing past, I eventually came to the lane halfway up which was my house. This lane was where the wealthy of our town lived. My place was a large 1920s semi that I kept in entirely authentic condition. Rather than replace the slender curved metal windows with brutish PVC as many others had done, I had kept the ones that remained and had restored them where they had been removed. Inside the house the honey waxed parquet floor was totally genuine and the door fittings and light switches were the original Bakelite.

In deliberate contrast my furniture was modern Italian, stylish items from the Memphis Group and Atalanta and in the living room was a Loewe plasma flat-screen TV complete with surround sound. I let myself in and lay down on the wooden floor.

About two and a half years ago Sage Pasquale's sister had married her husband; at that time he was employed as a vivisectionist at a laboratory outside Northampton and lived in a dead, silent village in the nearby countryside with the blackened shapes of his last two firebombed 4 x 4s still parked on the drive.

They held the party after the wedding in the hospitality suite of the laboratory, the disco only just drowning out the screams of monkeys with wires in their brains. Our gang put up in the big Edwardian rectory opposite the converted railway station where Sage Pasquale's anorexic sister and her fiancee lived. Now the rectory was a bed and breakfast hotel run by a disgraced couple by the name of Major and Mrs Marvin. Or rather it was Major Marvin who was disgraced, Mrs Marvin was just disgraced by marriage. Sage Pasquale's sister got drunk on a small glass of water, then she told us the story. 'Don't tell anybody,' she said emaciatedly, 'but the major was once something really important in Scottish tropical fish administration until he did something or failed to do something with a person or a fish or some money that meant he lost his job and they had to move four hundred miles to avoid the shame and they had to let out the big house they bought for bed and breakfast.'

In every room in the house there was either a stuffed fish of some kind or a picture of a fish on the wall. None of us had really noticed the Marvins the night before, simply checked in, unpacked our stuff and gone out again to the village pub for Sage Pasquale's sister's fiancée's stag night. But the next morning we all met up in the dining room to be served breakfast by the Marvins.

It was like being in a fish mausoleum so many stuffed *poissons* were on display. The six of us sat round a big table in a bay window out of which we could see Colin's Jaguar S, Sage Pasquale's BMW 735i, Siggi's Lexus IS 200 and my Range Rover filling up the gravel forecourt and denting the Marvins' herbaceous borders. Mrs Marvin had already been in and taken our orders for breakfast and the major had popped in for a stilted chat about what the fuck we were doing in his village.

A few minutes later Mrs Marvin returned, bringing in our breakfasts two at a time; as she was serving the second load Loyd suddenly started to act incredibly scouse.

'Eh luv,' he said to her, waving a bit of bacon about on the end of his fork, 'dis bacon is da biz, y'know worra mean.'

The rest of us picked it up in an instant. 'Oh, an'dem eggs,' said Colin, 'they look cracker.'

'Oh, dis is da gear dis brekkie,' said Sage Pasquale, who wasn't even from Liverpool but came from Harpenden.

'Dese eggs is friggin' ace, girl,' said Siggi.

When Mrs Marvin returned, stepping cautiously as if she were on the edge of a tank filled with poisonous puffer fish, with the last two breakfasts in her hands, Kate said, ''Ere, hon, could ya get da major to do us another couple a dem fantastic kippers? Dey're dead moreish, honest.'

I said, 'Yiz stars, Mrs M, you an'dat major yiz stars. We're gonna come 'ere on our 'olidays ain't we, mates? Fuck Aya Napa dis is da go.'

They all shouted their assent.

'Yere right der, Kelvin,' yelled Loyd. 'Mrs Marvin, we's gonna come'ere every year, won't dat be da fuckin' biz?'

I remembered as we drove away on the Sunday afternoon, after I'd written 'very nice' in their comments book, that the Marvins stood on the porch to see us off. In my rear-view mirror I saw the hard plaster smiles they had been wearing switch off with an almost audible click as my Range Rover crickled across their gravel and turned the corner into the lane.

At the time I'd thought it was a brilliant laugh rubbing the Marvins' faces in the fact that all their Eton, Cheltenham

Ladies, Oxford and the Scots Guards had brought them to this, serving fried food and kippers to a pack of grinning, thirty-year-old morlochs. We had laughed about it often between ourselves since then but now recollecting that weekend I felt ashamed; I thought the pack of us had been too cruel tormenting the poor old couple.

That night I searched through my office files until I found the number of the Marvins' house. I dialled it but an automated voice told me their phone had been disconnected.

The negotiations took three months for me to buy the land in Liverpool which would become what I was already calling in my own mind 'Kelvinopolis'. The city councillors I was dealing with would have liked to drag things out for a good deal longer but recently several of the leading Liverpool crime families, the Gorcis, the Pooles and the Mukes, had put it about that they were becoming unhappy with the levels of home help that their old mums were getting from social services, so the council needed to find extra money fast or the councillors knew they would be held to account and by a more unforgiving figure than the local government ombudsman.

Coming back on the Mersey Link train following the formal hand over of the site, an electrical storm hung like an airship over Liverpool Bay and the scent of lightning rippled through the long grass that grew unattended between the railroad tracks. A man came and sat uncomfortably close to me while relating in a high-pitched voice the violent abuse he'd suffered at the hands of a succession of priests. However, fortunately he had to get off at Aintree Station as he was planning to throw himself in front of a horse so it was quite an uneventful journey really.

Walking up the lane from the station I noticed that there was another cirKuss poster stuck in the window of the Station Hotel: it told me that *Clamdango!* had been such a success on their last visit that they'd brought it back for another two weeks, the run beginning the previous Monday.

On the doorstep of my house stood a teenage boy, tall and muscular with gingery blond hair cut en brosse, wearing a padded jacket, huge baggy jeans with a chain looping low from the back pocket to the front. As I approached a small red hatchback started up with a clatter and took off, driving fast away from me in a cloud of diesel smoke. 'I'm a bit early,' the boy said.

'Was that your mum?' I asked as I let him in, indicating the red car turning the distant corner of my lane on two wheels.

'Yeah.'

'She could have come in, said hello.'

'Yeah, she didn't want to.'

'Why not?'

'You know why. She thinks you're a cunt.'

Fifteen years ago when we'd found out the eighteen-year-old Paula was pregnant, her and Colin had had to work very hard to reassure us all. 'We're not going to let having a kid affect us going out,' they said.

'We can all still go clubbing,' they said.

'We can all still go on holiday,' they said.

'Well, all right,' we said, though we weren't entirely convinced. Colin and Paula would need to make a real effort to show us they were still fun people.

After uneasy congratulations, I asked, 'What's the kid going to be called?'

'Adom,' Paula replied.

'You mean Adam?' said Siggi.

'No, "Adom",' said Colin. 'It's the new thing all the parents are doing, to change just one letter of your child's name.'

'Oh, right,' said everybody.

It was a new thing that became an old thing very quickly and lasted for little more than a year: now if you came across a kid called 'Christike', 'Stanleg', 'Puter' or 'Margarot' you know they were born in 1988.

'Oh, go on and tell me what she really thinks,' I said to Adom, trying to laugh it off.

'No,' he replied solemnly, 'that would upset you too much.'

'That your stuff for the weekend?' I asked, indicating his backpack.

'Yeah.'

Once we were seated in the living room I said, 'So how you doing, Adom?'

He looked up, annoyed. 'You can call me Adam now: I changed it legally once Dad died, you know that.'

'Okay, sorry, I forgot.' His mother's attitude was still bugging me. 'Isn't she grateful to me for taking you so she can have a nice long weekend away in Worthing?'

'She thinks you're my godfather so you're supposed to do stuff like that.'

'Well, I was going to take you to a kindly prostitute when you was sixteen but apart from that I thought it was just a fashion thing, godparenting.'

'Well, it turns out it isn't,' he said unforgivingly. 'She says she lost you all twice, once when you all dropped her in favour of Dad and again when they was all killed.'

'Right,' I said. 'And er . . . how's the er . . . the Friends and Family Group going?'

'All right I guess,' he replied. 'I know you think it's odd because her and Dad were divorced that she's the secretary of the Friends and Family Group.'

'I did a bit at first but whatever helps I guess.'

Looking at me straight he asked, 'Did you know Dad . . . he still would come round by himself you know, secretly to see her, to sleep with her. Did you know that?'

Here, though, I think he didn't give me the jolt he wanted. 'Yeah, actually I did. Sage Pasquale's sister's husband phoned me up one night about six months before the accident and told me.'

'It doesn't matter now does it?' he said.

'Not really, no,' I replied. 'And are you, you know, okay?'

'Oh yeah, I'm absolutely fine.'

I made dinner for Adam and myself. Not being aware of how much teenagers ate and my own appetite having shrunk so much, I had to cook a whole second dinner before the kid was full. He then went upstairs and did his homework; once that was finished he came back down and asked politely if he could go out and meet his mates at a pub in town. I couldn't see why not; though he was only fifteen most of the pubs in town seemed exclusively for the use of fifteen-year-olds.

After Adam left the house seemed suddenly empty. I wandered about tidying up magazines and stuff. At about eleven o'clock I went into my cold empty garage, took the Marin mountain bike down from its bracket on the wall; using the remote control I clanked the garage door open and rode out into the night. Despite the cirKuss ground being dark and unlit, the tiny tent and the hulking sinister grey trucks all seemed intensely familiar. I had an idea where she might be; well, to be honest, when they'd been here three months before I'd come to the site several times at this time of night until I'd found where she was and I'd watched her from a distance hidden by the trees but never approached.

I rode my bike along the tarmac paths that traversed the muddy grass until in a small square car park bounded by rustic log fencing I glimpsed her. As before she was leaning on the fence smoking a cigarette. I got off my bike, negotiating it with great difficulty through a narrow gate – one of its pedals stabbed me in the leg as I did so – and wheeled it over towards her. I know I could have left the machine leaning against the other side of the log fence but felt that a man with a bike was somehow less threatening: like a man with a dog, nobody ever suspected ill of a man with a dog, unless it was one of those mad, dangerous dogs of course. Not that she seemed like a girl who was worried by much. Unmoving, she'd watched me wrestle my bike through the gate; now she said as I got near her, 'You have oil on your trousers.'

'Eh?' I asked, already flustered.

'From da bike. You have oil on your trousers.'

'Fuck!' I said.

'You could have left it on de other side.'

'Yeah, you're right.'

I noticed that her English had improved dramatically since I'd last seen her; now she spoke with very little trace of an accent.

'So where is your fancy car?' she asked. 'Did you lose it in a bet?'

'Oh, so you remember me then?' I replied, pleased and

blushing in the dark. I hadn't thought she would; it was nearly a year after all.

'Yeah, you had a car that was made in the place with all the lights and you were a lot fatter before; it suited you better I think, jolly fat man. You don't look so well now, thin, miserable man. What happen, was it the bet, did you lose everything in the bet as well as your car?'

'Oh, ah, no, not a bet . . . Well, I don't know if you recall I . . . ah came to see your show with a group of friends and, ah, the next time, ah . . . we were on our way somewhere, ah, they were, ah . . . all killed.'

She took this in without the usual expressions of regret that you got from most people. Instead she asked, 'What, by paramilitaries?'

'No, it was in a car crash.'

'Yeah, that happens too I guess.'

'Yeah, it does.'

'Bummer,' she said.

'Yeah, bummer,' I replied.

We were silent for a while then she said, 'Do you wish to join the cirKuss?'

'No, I don't think so. Why?'

'Well, you know, a lot of the people here in the cirKuss that they are in the same situation as you. Either, you know, they have to leave all their friends and family behind, where they come from, and they never see them again or you know everybody been killed.'

'Fuck, really?'

'Yeah, we don't get many letters from der postman here.'

'No, I suppose you wouldn't.'

'Den on de other hand the postman don't know where we are 'cos we move around so much, so maybe it's not so surprising. Probably post is mostly junk mail anyway and catalogues from Viking Direct.'

'Right.'

'Still is bad situation,' she said, 'having all your friends killed; that, you can never, never get over, no point in trying. You understand that?'

'I think I'm getting there,' I said.

'If you think that you're getting there . . . I don't suppose you are yet,' she sniffed, then went on, 'Many I think it sends crazy. But you know what is best outcome? Is a little like when you break leg and it is not set properly by drunken doctor. So it grow back crooked and it always will give you pain but you know you still able to hop about on it. So, you know, maybe in time you can get new friends and a new family but they always grow kind of crooked, you know what I mean? Not normal like before and they always give you pain and what you do, the way you act is not like before, is kind of crooked too.'

'Hopping about.'

'Sure, hopping about; before friends killed everything is like one foot in front of the other, normal, straight. And after is hopping about, sure. But, you know, you still getting around. That is main thing even if it is in mad fashion.'

'And that's the best outcome? Well, that's great,' I said. 'Maybe I'd rather go crazy instead.'

She laughed. 'You can't choose to go crazy, it either happen or it don't.'

There was another pause. I realised I found it was rather exciting to be talking to somebody who I didn't already know everything about. With my tight little gang there had been no surprises since somewhere in the early nineties and of course there would be no more. In fact, I thought, remembering the last time we'd met, I seemed to find out less about this girl the more I talked to her. In a soft voice that I thought sounded caring and sensitive I said, 'Can I ask? Is that what happened to you? Do your family . . . or are they?'

In a not unfriendly way she replied, 'Hey, pal, not so fast. You don't get to learn what happen to me. Not right now. Maybe at some other time. I'm a person not some sad story.'

Which seemed a bit mean since I'd been telling her my sad story. Still, I said, 'Sure, I'm sorry I asked.' Again we stood in silence for a while then I enquired, 'Can I ask you what your name is?'

She sighed. 'You wouldn't be able to pronounce it. In my language I guess it sound a little bit like "Georgina".'

'So shall I call you Georgina then?'

'No, don't call me that!' she asserted with a sudden burst of ferocity; reflected for several seconds then said, 'Call me Florence.'

'Florence?'

'Dat's right, call me Florence.'

'Hi, Florence,' I said. 'My name's Kelvin.'

She snorted through her nose when I said this.

Smiling myself, I asked, 'What's so funny?'

'Where I come from a "Kelvin" is . . . well, it's something funny.'

'What?' I asked, laughing too. 'Come on, tell me.'

She could hardly get it out through her giggling. 'A "Kelvin",' she said, 'a "Kelvin" is a telecommunications relay tower for land-based microwave transmissions.'

'Oh, right.'

'What do you call them here?'

'I don't know. I think telecommunications relay tower for land-based microwave transmissions.'

'Oh.' She paused. 'So anyway I think I go to sleep now.'

'Right. Okay.' Then I said in a rush, 'Look I was wondering would you like to go out some time, with me somewhere?'

'Well, I work at nights . . .'

'Sure, stupid, forget it,' I said.

'No, no, I'm just saying, the day would be better, like maybe next Tuesday.'

'Oh okay, great, where would you want to go then?' I suddenly couldn't think of anywhere on the planet.

'Well, der is a shop in Liverpool called Bell and Banyon – do you know it?'

'No, but I'm sure I can find it.'

'Great, well meet me here at maybe twelve and we can go and shop der and maybe do something afterwards . . .'

'Fantastic, twelve here then.'

'Twelve here den.'

I picked up my bike, wrangled it through the gate, getting more oil on my trousers, and cycled off along the path.

When I got home and looked up Bell and Banyon's address in the Yellow Pages I read in their half-page advert that they were the north-west's largest independent retailer of disabled and elderly products.

It was after midnight when I got home, Adam wasn't in yet. I waited in the living room for him watching TV and didn't hear his key in the door until half past one. I called out, 'I'm still up, Adam!' However I was disconcerted by the next sound which was a thump as if a body had fallen to the floor. Rushing into the hall I found the boy lying face down in the open doorway. 'Oh fuck, oh Christ, Adam!' I cried, turning the boy over: blood was running over his face, one eye was already puffy, purpling and closed and mucus ran in a stream from the boy's flattened nose, causing him to talk in a snuffling, gasping manner.

'They were laughing at me . . . his nephews,' he said, his one working eye staring into some scene of horror that he held inside his head. 'So we jumped them because there was more of us than them but they knew what they were doing . . . See, they wanted to do me because they knew who my dad was and they were winding me up because their uncle was out.'

'Who was out? Who was out?' I shouted.

'Fucking Sidney Maxton-Brown,' gasped the boy.

5

'Stomach cancer,' said Sidney Maxton-Brown, patting his abdomen contentedly.

'Really?' I queried.

'Yeah, fucking awful it were, I were down to like five stone and the pain, Christ! Four months they said I 'ad to live. So you know they let me out on parole like, on compassionate grounds, to die at home.'

'And then?' I asked.

'And then,' replied Sidney Maxton-Brown, 'it went away.'

'It went away?'

'That's right; the doctors couldn't believe it, "a miracle" they said I was, "almost unheard of" they said, but it went away. "In remission" is actually what they call it but I know it's gone for ever, you can tell some'ow, if it's inside your body or not. Of course I haven't really, you know, felt the need to inform the coppers or the court or anything, that it's gone. I mean I don't know whether they'd put me back inside but I'd certainly lose me disabled parking badge.'

When Adam came back from the pub all beat up and collapsed half in and half out of the hall, I left him only for the few seconds I needed to grab the phone and with trembling hands to dial 999. Again I was connected immediately, as I had been on the night of the big crash; the woman I spoke to might even have been the same one I'd spoken to on that evening. She told me the paramedics would be there soon and not to move the boy, so we sat in the open doorway, the summer breeze blowing over us, an older man holding a keening teenager in his arms.

The two of us passed most of the rest of the night in the casualty department of the town's general hospital amongst the wounded of a quiet Friday, the impalings, the clubbings, the stabbings, the gougings. To me none of the wounds looked real, rather I felt like I was in the middle of one of those historic re-enactments staged in the grounds of a stately home, this one representing the gory aftermath of some medieval battle. We liked to go and see those in the summer, me and my friends, to laugh at the divvies in their silly outfits, fat clerks from Bolton pretending to be soldiers in Napoleon's Imperial Guard.

I'd tried to phone Paula but her mobile wasn't answering and I didn't know the name of the boarding house where she was staying. After Adam was lethargically examined by a series of exhausted-looking young doctors and pronounced only superficially injured, we got a taxi home at five in the morning. Without saying another word the boy went to bed and stayed there till his mum arrived to take him home. I tried to explain what had happened, when she came rushing over in response to the hysterical answerphone message I'd left eighteen hours earlier, but she wouldn't let me speak, just angrily led him away.

Unexpectedly, then, I had the weekend to myself. While I could have gone walking on the moors or visited a steam fair in Parbold, what I did instead on that Saturday was sit on the couch and think. Afterwards I felt like I'd thought a whole lifetime of thoughts in a single day.

I recall, perhaps falsely, who knows, that I remained in exactly the same position, unmoving apart from the occasional spasm that rippled across my cheeks until the evening of that Saturday, until the streetlights came on, until the men and women from the surrounding houses returned from their weekend trips to the supermarket, the ski slope, the squash courts, and the smell of salad began to fill the evening air.

I sat on my couch and thought and thought and thought, the tumblers of my mind clicking over like the lock of an elaborate, well-lubricated Edwardian safe.

In the first hours my visions were all of revenge. One thing I was absolutely certain of was that affairs could not be left as they were: that this Sidney Maxton-Brown would somehow be allowed to escape even the vastly inadequate punishment the law had given him was simply not an option.

Something was going to be done, the only question was what. Some violent act could certainly be arranged; nobody got very far in the building game without understanding that an industry which encompassed sharp implements, quick-drying concrete, sudden profits, sudden losses, penalty clauses, an itinerant workforce that was inclined to settle disputes without reference to the small claims court, grinding, chomping, mashing machines and deep, deep, dark holes, occasionally did involve the odd abrupt disappearance in the middle of the night.

I knew, if I wanted to go down that road, that it would be possible to pay someone to have the tipper man kidnapped and tortured, or beaten up or just shot on his doorstep by a figure in a crash helmet. Of course you could never absolutely guarantee that things would go the way you wanted them to go. I discerned from things I'd heard that even big crime families like the Gorcis and the Mukes, with all their resources and their minds that looked at everything as an opportunity for crime, could come unstuck trying to kidnap rivals, intimidate prosecution witnesses, kill people who had spilled drinks on them in pubs and so on.

Also, if you started on that sort of violent retribution route then the other party or the relatives of the other party were capable of embarking on it too and it was already clear that Sidney Maxton-Brown came from the sort of tribe that didn't appreciate the other person's point of view, who wouldn't view a beating up as fair retribution for his evil behaviour.

Not to mention the moral angle, which nobody did much any more.

And somehow paying out a pile of money or calling in a load of favours simply to have somebody who had wronged you whacked seemed at the end of the day to be too . . . I don't know, it seemed to be too . . . unoriginal. A ten-year prison sentence and some flowers nailed to a fence had seemed an inadequate enough memorial to my five friends but a shabby hit was nowhere near what they were entitled to.

It wasn't in the night but round about teatime when I came to the conclusion that for all those reasons I didn't want to resort to violence and yet I knew that the most important thing in my life was that I needed to take revenge on Sidney Maxton-Brown. This revenge was to be my memorial to my friends and therefore it needed to be worthy of them, it needed to embody their qualities of originality, their humour, their thirst for great art. Through building their memorial I realised I was also hoping that my life might begin again.

What I wished for, I thought, was that Sidney Maxton-Brown should feel a little of the terrible pain, a fraction of the awful terror that my friends had felt as they died and that their friends and relatives experienced to this day. Except, I mused, even if you did kidnap and torture him he still wouldn't be feeling what they had felt; if you worked him over, if you pulled his fingernails out he'd still be feeling only his own pain. What was really desired, I reflected, was for Sidney to understand just some tiny part of what he had done, to comprehend even to the minutest degree the awful effect he had had on the lives of so many innocents. But how could a thing like that be achieved?

What was needed, I thought, was a way to prick a hole in the bubble of Sidney's biosphere of self-pity and let in the corrosive outside air. Yet how the hell could you make one person understand how another person felt?

I pictured my friends, thought about what it was that we did together; mostly we went and saw things. So I tried to remember all the performances we'd seen together. I tried to recall all the movies we'd seen, all the plays we'd attended, the computer games we'd played, the novels we'd read and what we'd learned from them.

Well, a lot of them had been crap and we'd learned nothing at all. I had kept the programmes of every play I'd ever seen; now flicking through them there were many nights at the theatre from which I could not recall a single detail. I mean what the hell was *Old Bollocks* at the Octagon Theatre Bolton, starring the late Michael Elphick that I apparently sat all the way through in March 1996? Or *Quonk*, at the West Yorkshire Playhouse, or *Stuvitsky's Rehearsal* at the Theatre Clwyd Mold. Somebody had spent a year writing these things, actors had been cast, sets had been built, I'd gone to see it and there wasn't an atom of memory remaining of what had gone on. What was the point? I thought about all the comedians we'd seen over the years with their banal unsights into the human condition: 'Men are like this, women are like that, isn't it annoying when your teapot . . .' I remembered the bit a lot of comedians did about what wimps men were, a bit that I'd laughed along with but now I thought, What men? Nelson Mandela, did he go all piteous when he got a cold while he was imprisoned on Robben Island? Rupert Brooke in the trenches? Victor Jara being tortured by the Chilean junta?

On the other hand my memory of some events we'd attended was more ambiguous. I thought about the last art exhibition that we had all been to together, at the Tate Liverpool. Sage Pasquale had said, 'Dan Flavin worked solely in neon tubes. Hundreds of ordinary coloured tubes in different groups and arrangements. Though Flavin was credited with being one of the creators of minimalism he once joked that he would rather it was called "maximalism".'

Though I looked grimly at the tubes and concentrated ever so hard and strove to find some meaning in it, all I kept thinking was, With all these neon tubes buzzing away has the gallery's electricity bill gone up? And secondly, How has the gallery coped with the different voltages? Because when I'd looked closely at the tubes I'd noticed that these were US neon tubes and seeing as the US was on 110 volts with 50 cycles A/C compared to the UK 240 volts system, did they have a different transformer for each artwork or one big transformer for the whole gallery? But then I thought, No, if they've put this stuff in this gallery and all these critics have praised it then there must be some worth in it. So I forced myself to look harder and then I did see meaning in it though I'm not entirely sure what it was, but the shapes were beautiful and the colours were pure.

None the less I did believe that there had been times when we'd undoubtedly been truly transported by something we'd seen; without any conscious introspection we'd all know right away that we were witnessing something profound. Such as the Protection Racket DJ'ing at Glastonbury, or when our book group had read Zhao Zhi Zhu's *When the Bamboo Flowers*: that was amazing. Bamboo only flowers once every hundred years and the book is a chronicle of four generations of one Chinese family between one flowering and the next, from the Opium Wars, the Boxer Rebellion, civil war, the Long March, the early years of communism, the Cultural Revolution, ending at the handover of Hong Kong. Those Chinese, man, they went through a lot; we were so moved by this saga that we tried to get the guy that delivered our sweet and sour pork to tell us his family's turbulent story, but he said they were all from Nottingham and nothing much had ever happened to them. There was that musical we saw based on Primo Levi's stories and of course the *Hats of the Pharisees* exhibition at the Royal Academy. Anyway, what I'm saying is that when we'd seen these things all of us had experienced a collective sense of having pushed through some curtain into a greater understanding of what it was like to be human.

Most of all, I remembered a weekend trip the six of us had taken to Amsterdam in 1999. Air miles from Liverpool Airport. We got there on a Friday evening, checked into our hotel then piled right out again, went round the drug cafés and had an Indonesian Rijsttafel. On the Saturday evening after a busy day of shopping for antiques at the

Spiegelwartier and a visit to Anne Frank's house, an indifferent meal at the Michelin-starred Excelsior, a sex show in the red-light district, we danced, high on MDMA powder till four in the morning at a club called Bunnies in the Leidseplein area. Having only had four hours' sleep Sage Pasquale forced us up at 8 a.m. so as to be first in line at the Van Gogh Museum. Tired and drugged and groggy, we paid our money and joined the crowds of tourists drifting through the stuffy concrete rooms. Sage Pasquale rented one of those tape and earpiece things so she was able to provide a running commentary on the paintings: she got quite angry at it and said why didn't they do a concealed version with one of those tiny transparent earpiece things so other people would think she was a tremendous authority on art history.

The pictures at the Van Gogh Museum were presented in chronological order so that slowly we were taken through the fevered illustrations to Vincent's sad, desperate, short life. From the muddy browns of *The Potato Eaters*, we travelled with him to Paris to the brighter, happier colours and Japanese influences of *Self Portrait At Easel*, then south we went to the house in Arles that he shared with Gauguin for a while and the painting of *Sunflowers* so powerful in the flesh that it transcended its too-copied life.

The last painting of all was *Crows in the Wheatfield*, the bleak dismal birds struggling to get off the ground like the painter's own black thoughts. Sage Pasquale, her voice cracking with sorrow, choked out, 'A few days after he finished this painting Van Gogh went into those same fields and . . . and shot himself . . .' She turned away from the painting to see the five of us were all weeping too, at what it was hard to say: for ourselves, for Vincent, because we'd taken too much ecstasy, who knows? 'Oh God, the poor man,' she said, then, 'Hold me, Kelvin,' so I took her in my arms and held her tight and Colin did the same with Siggi and Loyd with Kate till our tears had dried and it was time to get the shuttle bus to the airport.

At first I got excited by the idea that if I could somehow simply put this killer in front of great works of art then that would humanise him; it took only a few minutes for that notion to go cold, well, not cold but there was a sense I'd need something more. Just showing Sidney Maxton-Brown stuff or getting him to read stuff (if he could read) or watch stuff couldn't possibly be enough, there would need to be something else. What it was I couldn't think right now but I was confident it would come to me in time.

Monday morning I got on the phone.

A couple of times I had to put the handset down with shaking hands before being connected, but finally I managed to hold on to myself long enough until a young woman with a Lancashire accent said, 'Maxton-Brown Tipping.'

I told her my name then said, 'I'm a developer. I've got a job on in Liverpool that'll need big tipper work. I'd like to talk to the boss of your firm.'

'That'd be the Uncle,' she said.

'Can I come and see the Uncle then?'

We agreed on a time and a date towards the end of the week and she gave me the address of a farm about five miles outside our town.

The prospect of meeting with the man who had killed my friends lent the rest of the day an agitated quality. In a way I found myself welcoming this agitation, it felt healthy, like the pins and needles of blood returning to a limb that had been lain on for too long. I realised all round I was in for a funny week: not only was I wound up over my assignation with Sidney, there was my daytime date with Florence too.

She was waiting for me when I got to the common, standing in the same smoking spot where we had talked late on the previous Friday night.

I'd fallen in love before and I hadn't particularly liked it. It had felt like being an indoctrinated citizen of some country run by a terrible dictator; the object of my love had become the Beloved Leader, appearance flawless, morals perfect, beliefs exemplary, every dazzling utterance endlessly fascinating, every brilliant statement needing to be endlessly dissected for meaning and subtext. No matter whether I liked it or not, I knew as soon as I saw her that it was happening to me again: I experienced the tumbling sensation in my mind that told me my feelings for Florence had shown their papers to the border guards and had crossed over the barbed wire into the country of love.

One of the few ways I'd found to protect myself from total gawpishness was to look for defects in the girl's appearance and thus to diminish slightly her perfection.

I realised I'd never seen Florence in daylight so hoped perhaps to see some blemish in her skin but when I got up to her and kissed her on the cheek it was flawless like the rest of her. She looked a little smaller perhaps, but that was it and in fact her smallness made her seem even cuter.

For the ordinary civilian their body was merely something to go down to the shops in but for a performer such as Florence it was as if her body was a beautiful dress that she had just that minute put on; she was aware of every brush of its fabric against her, a beautiful dress that she knew staggered the onlooker and that she deliberately turned in the light so its diamonds and pearls sparkled and hummed.

On top of that the dress she was actually wearing was quite something too: an old-fashioned ballet skirt, layer after layer of black netting down to her knees with black satin petals laid on the top, a black Adidas top zipped up to her neck, black fishnet tights on her long legs and white Reebok trainers with a blue stripe down the centre.

When she saw me a big smile spread across her face and she jumped up and down with excitement, making her skirt bounce in harmony and making me smile too. I put my hands on her waist and kissed her on the cheek.

'Hi,' I said.

'Hi,' she said. 'I've been looking forward to seeing you this much.' And she spread her arms apart to indicate a huge amount.

'Me too.'

She took me by the hand and said, 'Before we go on trip, I want you to come and say hello to the rest of everybody.'

'Yeah okay, sure,' I replied reluctantly. 'Even Valery?'

She began to lead me towards the cirKuss tent. 'Especially Valery. You must understand Valery is my special friend. My buddy. He is from the next village to me back home, so he knows me like nobody. But I cannot stand it if you are not friends with Valery. Unlucky though he cannot speak nearly any English so he cannot tell you all the great things about me.'

'I hope I find them out for myself,' I simpered.

She took me across the tarmac showground into the big mouth and we entered the hot interior of the tent. Everybody I recalled from my previous visit seemed to be in there though quite why I couldn't discern; there seemed no reason for them to be inside the tent since they were all sprawled about on the benched seating or on the floor of the ring doing absolutely nothing at all. I felt like a fat family driving their shitbox saloon car tentatively into the lion enclosure of a safari park. All around me sinuous feline forms stared with cold eyes and slowly unwound themselves, sniffing the air and wondering whether I was edible or not.

Still, Florence's happiness was contagious; it made me grin idiotically just to look at her as she dragged me from one bizarrely named person to another. 'Glinka this is Kelvin, Pnnnngg and Bvvvvxxx say hello to Kelvin, Kelvin this is my good friend Toast Arrangement . . .' It dawned on me that I was being shown off, that for some reason this stunning woman was proud of me as she introduced me one after another to her fellow cast members. I shook hands with various Asians, Africans, assorted shades of Levantine and Slav, none of whom seemed to display the enthusiasm for me that Florence felt.

I also got the impression that unlike Florence not many of the other performers had made much effort to learn English, that they lived in their own enclosed world and rarely ventured outside it.

Finally we came to Valery. Florence ordered me, 'Kelvin, say again how you are sorry to Valery.'

Eager to please her I said, 'Valery, I'm sorry I threw your ball away that time.'

At first the clown just mumbled something under his breath in a foreign language but Florence snapped a string of clacking words at him and surprisingly the big man rose and took me in a tight embrace. I hugged him back but then unseen and unheard by anyone else Valery whispered in my ear, 'You stay away her.'

Oh, fucking brilliant, I thought as I unwrapped myself from the clown. He fancies her and he's fucking jealous. Then, surprising myself, I realised I felt really sort of pleased that someone was jealous of me.

Unaware that things weren't now perfect, Florence took my hand and announced to the cirKuss folk, 'We're going to Liverpool!'

Outside I said, 'Shall we get the train?'

'No train!' she said, pointing to one of the grey-painted vehicles ranged alongside the tent. 'We go in my truck.'

The vehicle she indicated was one of the smaller four-wheel drives but still it rode high on huge all-terrain tyres, there was a split windscreen driver's cab complete with machine-gun cupola in the roof hunkering behind a long tapering bonnet. Mounted on the back of the heavy steel ladder chassis was a separate box body, its roof adorned with powerful auxiliary spotlights; wooden steps led up to a padlocked metal door set in its side.

'You want to see where I live first?' she asked.

'Sure,' I said.

She scampered ahead of me up the steps, unlocked the door and stepped inside. I followed her, subconsciously expecting something like the interior of the caravan my parents had rented for years on a site just outside Llandudno – frilly cushions, cupboards up the walls, narrow foam banquettes and the smell of powerful toilet chemicals so that I was unprepared to see . . . a room. Simply that, a room with an old-fashioned couch and matching moquette-covered armchair, standard lamp with fringed shade in one corner, paintings of mountain villages, lakes and forests on the walls, rag rugs over the floor, telly in the other corner.

Florence giggled at my amazement. 'Is proper living room. I don't want to live in caravan, I'm not fucking gypsy or Dutch tourist. I don't cook so no cooker and for toilet there is always fields, so no toilet. I don't want to sleep with a bucket of shit, you know.'

'Who would,' I said.

'Exactly, so now we go to Liverpool.'

We climbed back out of the body of the truck, Florence locked the door and folded the stairs away underneath. Then she skipped round to the left-hand driver's side of the cab, opened the door and jumped straight up, twisted in mid-air and dropped into the driver's seat. On the other side I climbed like a drugged monkey swinging off various grab handles, projecting bolts, obscure protuberances and metal steps, my shoes slipping on the wheel rim until I clumsily managed to haul myself gasping into the passenger seat of the high cab.

Florence started up the big diesel by pressing a red button on the metal dash, stomped on the enormous clutch pedal, wrestled the truck into first gear with both hands and, hauling on the enormous thin-rimmed wheel, steered the truck out of the cirKuss ground. The sight of this beautiful young woman, her whole body bending to the machine, sent a shiver of desire corkscrewing up my legs through my trunk and out the top of my head.

Noticing this spasm she asked, 'Are cold? The heater is slow to . . .'

'No, not cold, no,' I said. 'I, erm . . . haven't been in a vehicle since the . . . you know, the . . .'

'You scared?'

'In this thing? No, just memories kicking me around.'

Indeed as we rolled slowly down the slip road to join

the M57 (we had to go slow at first because one lane was entirely taken up by a long ragged trench, overflowing with rainwater and garbage but no workmen – I actually don't think it was one of mine), then picked up speed with the engine note building to a stentorian cackle, the cab and body began pitching and creaking to such an extent that conversation became too much of an effort and I found myself relaxing in the bouncing seat and watching her drive, so that after a while a benign calm settled over me and I felt more at peace than I had done for a long time.

She left the truck taking up two parking spaces at the top of London Road and from there we walked into Liverpool town centre.

I said, 'So you know this place is the north-west's largest independent retailer of disabled and elderly products; you don't think it's a juggling shop or anything?'

'That's right. I know what it is.'

'So what are you going there to buy, stuff for people back home who've been like wounded in the civil war?'

'No, why would I do that?' she asked. 'I'm buying stuff for me.'

'For you? But you're not disabled and elderly.'

'Not now I'm not,' she said, then after a pause went on, 'Look, you read car magazines right, man with car like that reads car magazines?'

'Sometimes . . . not now, I used to.'

'Well, in car magazines they always say that when you want to buy speciality car best time to do it is out of season when they are not so in demand. So if you've got your heart set on Mercedes convertible much better you do a deal in winter when nobody else is thinking about convertible car. Same if you want four-wheel drive you go down to the Land-Rover showroom in the height of summer when nobody thinking about driving in the mud. So now I think that one show at the cirKuss I will have bad fall in the ring or if not I will certainly be old one day then will need walking-stick or wheelchair or what you call that frame thing?'

'Zimmer frame.'

'Zimmer frame, yes. Now in those shops, where they sell disabled stuff they used to having people in who are all sick and weak, they not going to do a deal with those people but I go in there and I say, "Hey, look at me. I don't need your stuff, do me a good bargain!" and they will: it's guaranteed.'

I wasn't so sure that was how things worked, but considered her way of thinking about the sweetest thing anybody had ever said; it gave me a mild hard on. I said, 'I'm not certain you can haggle in a medical goods showroom.'

'Oh, everybody haggle,' she stated emphatically as we turned through the double doors of the north-west's largest independent retailer of disabled and elderly products. For a while we were left unattended to browse and Florence scuttled about with adorable enthusiasm poking at walking-sticks and vibrating seats and wheelchairs and adult incontinence pants (organic or non-organic) with squeals of delight. She was particularly taken by one of those giant big-foot heated slippers that a whole person can sit in. 'Oh, dis would be great for my truck,' she said. 'I would be so snug in there.' And I wanted to fuck her right there and then, pulling her tights down and bending her over a display of commodes or perhaps I thought we could do it inside the big slipper.

Eventually a middle-aged man in a greasy suit wandered

over to us just as Florence was trying out the brakes on a wheeled Zimmer frame. 'Good afternoon, can I help you?' he asked dubiously.

'Sure,' replied Florence. 'I am interested in buying many things for myself, okay? But before we talk about that I would like you to watch this.' And so saying she performed a series of five somersaults down the central aisle of the shop, ending the last one with a handstand; she balanced upside down for a few seconds before shooting herself upwards, turning over in mid-air and landing in the splits. Finally she sprang back up and took a deep bow by bending right over, her head sweeping the floor. 'And look,' she said as she came back up, indicating the spot on the floor where her legs had been spread, 'I didn't pee myself.'

'I thought everybody haggle,' Florence said angrily as she stomped down the street with me behind her struggling to keep up.

'Apparently not.'

'Stupid motherfuckers.'

'You know, thinking about it, you might have had a narrow escape.'

'In what way?'

'You might have bought all that stuff then it might be your bad luck to live to be a hundred and twenty years old with no injuries or infirmities.'

She stopped and said with vehemence, 'No I can't think like that.'

'Why not?' I asked.

She considered for a moment. 'Okay. Do you know why most old people are so grumpy? I tell you. Because old age come as a big shock to them, dey not expecting it at all. One day to them dey running about climbing trees then the next day dey got crumbly bones syndrome. My plan is that if you think about being old all the time and you expect the worst all the time then it won't be such a big shock to you when it happen.' Then she said thoughtfully, 'You know you're lucky, you already got a head start in knowing what it's like to be old person.'

'How's that?' I asked.

'Well,' she said, 'all your friends are already dead.'

She took my arm. 'Is your home-town?'

'Yeah.'

'So show me important places for you, show where little Kelvin used to go.'

So we walked around town and I pointed out to her where the superclub Cream had been and I talked about the beginning of places like Cream and Ministry and the anarchy of clandestine rave culture. I showed her where Liverpool's first branch of Next had opened, where I'd bought my first Nintendo, the pub where I'd seen my first alcopop, the chip shop I'd been in when I'd heard about Thatcher's resignation and how people had danced in the streets, the time Ant and Dec had come to open the new branch of HMV records and a madman had shouted obscenities at them. Then she told me she had to get back to our town for her evening show.

An hour and a half later as she dropped me at the end of my road she said, 'Sunday night is last show we're doing here, there is always party afterwards, you want to come?'

'Yeah, sure, that'd be great.'

'Thank you for my lovely day,' she said, then she kissed me on the cheek before I clambered backwards out of the cab, burning my hand on a hot exhaust pipe that I tried to hold on to.

Two days later I went to meet Sidney Maxton-Brown. As the taxi took me across the flat black cabbage-stinking farmland the driver was saying, '. . . so I never knew me real parents but me foster dad wasn't too bad I suppose, at first, until he got back from the Falklands that is, that's when the delusions started. I had to go to school wrapped in Bacofoil and fuse wire which meant that the bullying which hadn't been too bad started to get . . .'

Off the A road we turned, down a long high-hedged lane that took us suddenly past a ten-foot-high studded black metal gate set in a towering bramble and elder hedge. The driver braked and without for a second interrupting his Dostoyevskian narrative, reversed to skid backwards into the entrance. This abrupt arrival set howling an indeterminate number of big dogs. 'I'm not fucking going in there,' mumbled the driver, who only seconds before had been telling me that every second of every day all he wanted to do was to lie down and die, but now seemed all of a sudden to have discovered a wish to live.

So I paid him off, watched him drive away and stood alone on a sunny afternoon in front of a metal gate in a country lane waiting to meet Sidney Maxton-Brown. There was a steel entryphone set into a pillar at the side of the gate. I pressed a button, and after a few seconds a girl's voice answered. I said, 'I've come to see Sidney Maxton-Brown.'

'Right,' she replied. 'You've come to see the Dad.' And with a zizzing sound the gate swung open.

While the unseen hounds continued to bay, I was presented with a vision that caused me to laugh out loud. Straight ahead across a patch of worn grass about the size of a tennis court was the most gigantic log cabin I'd ever seen. I had read about them in building trade magazines, complete kits built in Canada or northern United States, shipped over and assembled in situ, but had never actually stood in front of one until now.

This was two storeys high, with a massive glass prow front in the centre and to onc side a wide pine staircase leading from the grass up to a wooden deck supported on pillars running around the entire front of the house at the first-floor level.

At the top of the staircase stood the man I supposed was Sidney Maxton-Brown. Remember he had not been brought up into the court when the trial was suspended and I had not returned to witness him being sentenced so I didn't know what he looked like. In the intervening days since making the phone call I had many times imagined what this man might look like: one of my images had been of an overweight, balding, thick-spectacled man looking all of fifty-five years old, wearing a green cardigan over greasy shirt and green pants that his belly had turned over at the top to show his white underpants and the grimy grey trouser lining, and I'd been entirely right, except his trousers were brown. Next to him stood a woman of about the same age; she had flat, greasy, muddy-coloured hair streaked with grey, a scoop-necked turquoise T-shirt and a grubby floral skirt whose elasticated waist rested just below her flabby flat breasts.

Several times in and out of the building game I had met people who each morning splashed on the authentic perfume of evil. Men from whom you wanted to run every second that you were laughing and joking and dancing in their company; for instance most members of the Gorci and the

Muke families that I'd been at school with made me feel exactly like that, even though I'd always been extremely popular with all of them. One of the conversations me and my friends had had every few years was what our special gift was; we thought each of us had one. Sage Pasquale's special gift was that she never ever stepped in dog shit; she could be walking down a pitch-black alley at night but somehow her foot would always swerve away from any pile of canine crap lying in ambush. Colin could invariably tell what people's pets were called, Loyd could always guess a person's shoe size; they all agreed that my gift was that I got along with absolutely everyone. I supposed that quality must come in useful when you were about to meet someone who had killed your five best friends. Except that I didn't think I was like that any more, that friendly fellow had gone. Well, I needed to call him up again for this task.

The sulphurous stench drifting from the adjacent cabbage fields even conspired to lend the air a demonic odour so that the man standing at the top of the pine staircase, the man who had ruined my life with his indifference, seemed even more utterly banal than if he'd been encountered under more normal circumstances. Behind Sidney was a thin silent girl of perhaps fifteen holding a baby and a young boy and girl with runny noses holding the older woman's skirt. Fighting the simultaneous impulses both to run and to launch myself at the man's throat, I waved and smiled, Sidney waved back and I mounted the stairs to meet him.

'All right?' said Sidney in a thick Lancashire accent. 'The is me daughter Susam and me wife Barbara' (the smaller youngsters never rated an introduction). 'I thought we'd have a bid of lunch while we talked so sid down, sid down.'

'Yes, you boys sid down and I'll ged you dinner,' said Barbara.

On the verandah there was a long pine table on which had been laid two places facing each other; alongside each plate was a small quarter-litre bottle of fizzy pop. The women and children went off inside the log house and me and Sidney sat at the table.

'This is quite a housc,' I said.

'Oh aye, the "Wounded Knee" model. 'Ad it shibbed over from Canada, not strictly allowed to build a house on this land zoned for agriculture but I got away with it, claimed it was an ostrich fattening shed, temporary agricultural structure see? Got a EC subsidy for the ostriches as well.' Behind his thick-lensed brown spectacles Sidney's single good eye shone with glee while the other faulty one stared off towards the tree line with a cynical and bored insouciance as if to say to me, 'I know what you're up to, darling, you can't fool me.'

'Now I've got four bedrooms,' Sidney continued. 'Sure I've got to keep an ostrich in one of them but it's a small price to pay. Double height living area, kitchen up here and the offices of me haulage firm downstairs; that's not strictly legal either but you can tie the council up for years with appeals so they usually give up.' As Sidney talked, a litany of planning wheezes, bribed officials, unsound structures, my gaze wandered; from this first-floor eyrie I could see off to the left in a slashed and burned patch of ancient woodland and rare orchids, five extremely battered four-axle tipper trucks of various vintages and makes, a Mercedes four-wheel drive and a Jaguar with, for some reason, Monaco number plates. These were not the vehicles that really caught my eye however, because parked in a neat row at right angles to the civilian trucks were a couple of German World War Two Kubelwagen scout cars, a German half-track and, looming over them all, the long barrel of its 75mm cannon casting a lengthy shadow across the grass, was a 1943 Panther Mark 4 tank. All of these were painted in grey camouflage and carried the twin lightning strike symbols of an SS Panzer Regiment.

'Interested in my liddle army are you?' said Sidney, following my gaze.

'I don't know many people that have their own Panther Mark 4 tank.'

'You know your armour,' Sidney said approvingly. 'Oh aye, I'm in one of them historical re-enactment groups, the first British SS Leibstandart Division. We do World War Two battles and our massacre of Polish civilians is very popular. There's actually a group who specialise in being massacre victims, they do some lovely pleading for their lives. I don't want you to think it's anythin' fascist mind, we've got a couple of darkie lads in our regiment . . . come to think of it they might be a bit fascist, certainly don't seem too keen on the Jews; still, they god their own Mark 6 Tiger in lovely condition, armed with the rare 88mm gun it is.'

'Black SS officers?'

'Well, they wear big helmets and goggles to cover them up so the audience can't see they're darkies. We're all 'oping to go to western Russian next year to re-stage the Battle of Kursk, the largest tank battle of all time, against collectors of Soviet tanks.'

'What, Russians? I'm surprised they can afford it.'

'No, no, not Russians, they're nod interested, Americans mostly. The largest regiment of Red Army T34s, the Ninth Guards Armoured is actually based in Los Angeles.'

* * *

Barbara Maxton-Brown served us lunch, which was a single pork chop garnished with half a pear lying on a plate accompanied by a pile of hummus, boiled carrots, some Chinese noodles and next to it tinned peas mixed with tartare sauce served in a porcelain teacup.

From time to time while we ate and talked another different teenager with I suppose a different baby would wander out on to the verandah then go back inside and some other little ones would wander in a line across the spartan grass as if in a mini version of one of Sidney's re-enactments.

Since I had conceived it, my plans for Kelvinopolis had grown as I realised that my way to forming a relationship with Sidney Maxton-Brown was to get him involved in its construction. I needed there to be such a large amount of rubble and dirt that required shifting that I could keep him working for me for a long time and I wanted it to be such a large tempting job that he would be forced to put up with all the strange things I might ask him to do. I said, 'Now this development is six terraced streets, thirty houses each side in a street; we'll strip out every house which should be enough rubble for two twelve-yard tipper trucks. I'll pay one hundred and eighty-five pounds per truck. It's going to be at least a one-year contract: there'll be site waste to shift as well as the rubble stripped out from the houses. That's not all though. We're going to demolish the central streets so there'll be a big open area that I'm going to plant an eco forest in. Now you probably know the thing every upscale development needs is a water feature: there's no canal nearby and the river's two miles away so I'm going to dig my own. I'm going to call it the River Anfield. That means there'll be a lot of soil from that that'll need taking away. Of course you'll have to pay dump fees out of the price but it's still a tidy profit.'

'It's an even tidier profit if you fly tip one load in foor,' simpered Sidney Maxton-Brown.

'Well, that's up to you,' I replied. 'But isn't fly tipping a bit risky these days?'

'Oh, don't you worry about that,' said Sidney. 'I know an out-of-the-way place. I mean, nobody visits those national parks anyway.'

So far so obvious. I had already figured out that one of the many corners, roundabouts and contraflows that Sidney Maxton-Brown would cut would be the avoidance of landfill fees by a bit of fly tipping: he would simply unload his trucks at any quiet spot he could find.

In anticipation of this I had already spoken to the boss of the reputable quality firm that usually handled my tipping. 'So what you're saying,' said the incredulous boss, 'is that you want me to pick up the rubble from the job that this cowboy will be fly tipping and take it to the proper dump.'

'That's right.'

'And you'll pay top rate for this?'

'Two hundred pound a truck.'

'But I'm not getting the job itself.'

'Well in a manner of speaking you are since you'll be taking a fair portion of the waste from the job to the tip.'

'That's fucked up.'

'Look, all right,' I said. 'I promise I'll also find another better, bigger job for you somewhere else. Satisfied?'

'No, not really, no. It's fucking mad.' A thought struck the contractor. 'Here, you're not having a nervous breakdown are you?'

'No,' I said, 'nothing so simple.'

Over dessert of digestive bisuits, whipped cream and Smarties Sidney said, 'Kelvin, I have to tell you that I recently served a term in prison.'

'Oh really?' I said, acting all innocent. 'What for?'

'A miscarriage of justice,' replied Sidney.

'Really, how come?' I said, twisting a fork out of sight under the table to stop myself stabbing him with it.

'Pure and simple, I was involved in a road accident where some people god accidentally killed, yet it was me got put in prison. See I never set out to kill those people, now how can it be a crime if I never set out to kill them? A crime is beating up pensioners or those sick bastards who go around molesting little kiddies that's what makes me mad, that's who the police should be after, nod somebody like me. All I do is I put my family first but everybody does that, don't they? I try to make a little money, to get by, to put food on my family's table, to pay for my daughter's operation . . . if she ever needs one that is.'

'So have they let you out on appeal or something?' I enquired, and it was at this point that Sidney told me about his lucky stomach cancer.

'I assume you're still banned from driving,' I said to stop himself tearing the haulier's lying, self-righteous throat out with my hands. 'So who does your driving now that you're banned?'

'Well, I use the nephews sometimes, but between you and me I'm still driving meself' – here he became heated – 'even though, even though, and the courts never took this into account, I've been suffering flashbacks since the crash. Well, I think they're flashbacks, they're a bit too short to tell really, somethin' to do with a field and some mud and a donkey as far as I can sort it out. I mean all the family say I should apply for compensation like they tell you to on the telly but I wouldn't do that, Kelvin, I'm no freeloader. Sidney Maxton-Brown pays his own way in the world.'

'So,' I persisted, 'you're still driving?'

'Oh aye, what am I supposed to do living out here? I gotta drive, ain't I, how can I ged about otherwise? It's victimisation to make a man with cancer . . . well, I always thought it was victimisation, whatever. I'm not going to get caught, am I? There's not much chance of the coppers checking, is there? Especially since I keep to the quiet roads. You ever been stopped? I certainly 'aven't and I been driving like a right cunt on many an occasion.'

'That'll be eight quid, mate,' demanded the taxi driver (not the same one as before) who dropped me back at my house. Then, 'I've always wanted to be a horse. I feel my whole life has been an empty lie because of it, I wish somebody would put a saddle on me and ride me through the . . . two quid change, there you go.'

I phoned Paula as soon as I got inside.

'Oh, it's you, what do you want?' she snapped.

Unable to come straight out with it I lied. 'I was just ringing to find out how Adam is . . . You know, since that night.'

'How do you think he is? I fucking wish you hadn't let him go to the fucking pub.'

'But you let him go to the pub all the time,' I whined.

'I know but I trusted you to look after him, you should have more sense.'

'So how is he?' I persisted, now suddenly needing to know.

She sighed. 'Well, since you asked, not too good. He hasn't gone back to school, he's really moody and he's been hanging round with all these losers in the neighbourhood. They've nicked his mobile phone and he pretends not to care.'

'Oh . . . er . . . oh.'

'Does that make you feel better?'

'No, not really, I dunno, maybe he'll straighten out, kids do.'

'And kids don't. Was there anything else?'

'Yes actually. Look, I wanted to talk to you about that Sidney Maxton-Brown.'

Here came the other element in my plan – to try and make the tipper driver live in a moral universe, a universe where his actions always had consequences.

Anger crept into her voice. 'You know the the police never told us he was out. I mean I'm glad the bastard is dying but the coppers' first response was to make feeble threats to arrest Adam and his mates 'cos it was them who had initially asssaulted Sidney's nephews. The Friends and Family have been raising holy shit with them; they're desperate now to make amends.'

'Well, that's good because get this,' I told Paula. 'Somebody told me they'd seen him and he's driving again, cars and trucks. I think the authorities would be eager to make amends by ensuring that that doesn't continue, don't you think?'

'That bastard! That fucking bastard,' she shouted. 'He won't be doing much driving. I'll make sure of that. Thank you for that, Kelvin. You know it made us feel powerless to know he was out, at least to stop him driving will be something.'

'Yeah, that's something.'

'It'll be a year you know since the . . . since the . . . next week, we're holding a sponsored swim, will you be coming?'

I said, 'I'll think about it.'

6

A crescent moon hung over the cirKuss ground. The grey wagons had been formed into a sort of town square, in the centre of which the performers and stage hands queued to get their pay for the week. Behind a pine trestle table one of the older clowns took notes out of a tin box and handed them over with an ungracious grunt. Florence had whispered to me as we sat on the steps up to her truck, me feeling like a conspicuous intruder, 'See Cronko the Clown, he is boss; the older ones say it was the same in Soviet circus days, clown was always boss and clown was always KGB. See now it all makes perfect sense that nobody likes clowns. I suppose all American clowns are CIA.' Then she skippingly took her place in line. Tonight Florence was wearing tight camouflage pants low down on her hips to show the curve of her lower belly, a short olive-green top that painstakingly outlined her breasts and big polished black army boots.

As I admired her lovely behind I thought about the eight girls I'd had sex with: it struck me there'd always been some flaw in their physical make-up; say they would have a wonderful pretty face and terrific upper body but then it would end in one thick stumpy leg and one chopstick thin one, or she'd have great tits stuck on one of those rippling bony chests, or a perfect body but hair like Ken Dodd's. This hadn't stopped me being in love with several of them and in fact a girl with the perfect arse but a neck like a WWF wrestler had broken my heart.

I worried that if I had sex with Florence for the first time tonight would I get the full benefit of seeing her flawless face and body? The problem, I realised, was that you can't get far enough back if you are in the process of fucking them to appreciate what they look like: what you ideally need, I thought, is a cock that is, say, seven foot long, though obviously you would only insert the first foot or so but then with a seven-foot cock you'd be able to get far back enough to get a good look at them and to relish their body while you were doing them. Of course with such a long cock you'd have nothing to do with your hands, you wouldn't be able to fondle anything unless your arms were also seven foot long but that would be ridiculous.

Once everyone was paid, from out of their trucks women began to carry large pots of hot spicy food which they laid out on the trestle table. A lot of the men lounged about pouring viscous drinks for each other from clear glass bottles with no labels on them, but other more industrious males threw together instant barbecues out of bricks and twisted wire on which they were soon cooking skewered cubes of meat, red peppers and chunks of onion. In the meantime a couple of the younger men had set up twin record decks hooked up to huge speakers from the cirKuss PA; they began by playing Coldcut featuring Lisa Stansfield, followed by KLF 'What Time is Love?' then a further string of hits from my teenage years.

Florence had conspicuously taken no part in the catering; instead she had lounged beside me on the steps of her truck with a vaguely sneering expression on her face. A couple of times older women seemed to address sarcastic remarks at her in a variety of languages to which she would spit back short epithets. At one point, from across the square Valery seemed to try and approach her but a girl with long red hair ran over, caught him by the arm and dragged him reluctantly backwards while her eyes shone hatred at a simpering Florence. I felt like I was an extra in one of those giant open-air productions of *Carmen* that we'd seen at Earls Court back in the mid 1990s.

Except the soundtrack for this show was from the early days of acid house rather than Bizet. Even before all the food was ready there had been a brief knife fight between two acrobats and a few minutes later the red-haired girl ran diagonally across the plaza weeping, with her mane streaming out behind her like a fighter jet on reheat. 'Is always fucking like this,' said Florence, then, ignoring further pointed remarks from fellow cast members, she pushed her way through the crowd at the pine table, now piled its whole length with stews, salads, grilled fish, hunks of bread, piles of rice and cracked wheat. Taking two plates, she loaded them with food and brought them back to me. 'Let's go inside to eat,' she said. As I mounted the steps I saw, emerging purposefully from the shadows, the acrobat who had lost the fight; in his hands he held an AK 47 assault rifle.

We both sat on the floor, Florence with her back against the couch, me leaning on the armchair as we ate our food.

I said, 'Quite a party out there.'

'Yeah, first fifty times is fun,' she replied, 'then it start getting on your nerves. Those people got a lot of problems, it makes them kinda tiring.'

'How do you mean?'

'All this passion all the time. Crying and fighting and stealing things from shops. When you live in the middle of it it's exhausting. Nobody here can simply get themself something like an index-linked pension for old age: they have to buy a big diamond from a Chinese man in Newcastle, then their brother steals the diamond, then turns out diamond is fake so two brothers get together to kill Chinese man in Newcastle.'

'That's just hypothetical, right?'

'Sure, imaginary scenario but you get the picture?'

'Yes, but maybe their behaviour is because of the terrible things that happened to them . . . to all of you.'

'Oh, all that was years ago, they need to get over it,' she said indifferently.

I thought, She pretends she's not damaged but I'm sure deep inside there's some terrible pain, and this made me want to have sex with her more than ever.

Inside the van the lighting came only from the fringed standard lamp. We both put our food down and I slid across the carpet to Florence. I took her in my arms and we began to kiss, our faces greasy with food. I felt like a teenager on a date years ago when I'd got a girl in my parents' front room with the gas fire going, rolling around on their patterned carpet. A while later as I came inside her, from outside there was a volley of rifle shots and some high-pitched screaming.

It was a warm early autumn day in Kelvinopolis as its progenitor, that's me, turned his face to the sun and waited for Sidney Maxton-Brown to appear for our first site meeting. This was a month after our initial lunch at the log cabin. The trucker was forty minutes late arriving but I was happy to spend the time walking my streets, making my plans. Finally Sidney appeared looking preoccupied in the passenger seat, his grumpy-looking wife at the wheel of the Mercedes four-wheel drive. As they rolled into the empty street I could see he kept staring over his shoulder, looking out of the back window in a distracted fashion. Sidney got out of the car, shook hands with me and as his wife bounced the ML up on to the pavement and took off, said, staring back towards the main road, 'Sorry we're late like, there was a huge bloody crane blocking off both lanes of the East Lancs road with no bastard working on it that I could see. That wasn't it though' – looking nervously around him once more – 'I think they've gone.'

'Who?' I asked.

'Fucking coppers. There was a Lancashire unit followed us from me farm and they handed over to a Merseyside vehicle at the city limits.'

'I thought you said the coppers didn't bother you?'

'They don't . . . didn't, I should say, but it was the strangest thing, the day after I saw you I think it was, I was on me way to a bit of hare coursing over Parbold way, on a tiny back road, when I looks in the mirror and there's a bleeding cop car. I couldn't fooking believe it, pulled over by the sodding police. They knew I was a disqual . . . managed to give them a yarn about me being on me way to urgent chemotherapy and all the nephews falling ill at once, but they said I was being watched and if I was found driving again for any reason whatsoever I'd be back in Walton Jail.'

'Fuck, that's bad luck,' I said. 'What are you going to do?'

'Dunno.' He looked genuinely upset. 'I've got to get

around. It's bin a nightmoor this past month, the wife and the nephews driving me everywhere.'

As if I'd just thought of it I said, 'Have you ever considered a bicycle?'

'A bike? Fook off!'

'I don't drive, I ride a bike.'

'Oh sorry, mate. No offence but I never thought of it, bikes are for kids like.'

'Not any more Sidney, you can get real quality machines, disc brakes, full suspension, stuff like that.'

'Er . . . right.' He looked around. 'So it's quite a site this; you should make a few bob from these places.'

'I suppose so,' I replied indifferently.

'You suppose so?' he exclaimed. ''Aven't you done cost benefit analysis, resale projections?'

'Naw, I don't bother with any of that, I think if it feels right—'

'You're fookin' mad!' he shouted angrily, then tried to turn it into a joshing thing by added on a strange chortling laugh, 'Gnooorft . . .'

I didn't wish to let such a useful philosophical point go so I said calmly, 'Look at me, Sidney, look at how rich I am, look at the size of the things I can do and I do them without ever, ever, thinking about how I do it. You never know, I might give some of these houses away to strangers I meet on a ferry or something.'

'You'll get took,' he said.

'Hasn't happened yet,' I said. 'I'm going to do loads of landscaping here, water features, artworks all over the place.'

'Yeah, but that'll just jack up the value,' he stated, at last seeing some greed in my actions.

'Maybe, that's not why I'm doing it. Immanuel Kant said the only truly moral act was one that brought you no benefit.'

'Well, he'd have to be nice to people with a name like that,' said Sidney.

Then we walked round the site and I showed him where his loads of rubble and soil would come from, telling him enthusiastically of my plans, the trenches that would be dug for sewers and services, the houses that were going to be demolished, the course of where the River Anfield would run, the areas that would need to be levelled and the others where gentle hills were to be created. Sidney's response to all this nascent beauty was to try and jack up his price.

Those involved in what's called groundworks – demolishing, digging, levelling – have always occupied the rougher end of the building trade. I suppose they lack the romanticism of the rest of us since they destroy rather than build. Therefore I wasn't surprised when Sidney said, 'We've got a problem here, Kelvin. I hadn't realised there were so many 'ouses around the edge of the site, the access is worse than I thought. I mean if I lose a load in the street or one of my trucks clips an 'ouse the insurance will be 'orrendous and where you're demolishing there's cellars that'll be left and a truck could fall in; there's a definite danger of contiguous collapse of 'oles. Then there's the soil, this soil is terrible poisoned. There's been dye works round here since the Middle Ages so there'll be mercury, cadmium, God knows what.'

Smiling and polite, I replied, 'One, Sidney, I've looked at every drawing of this area since the Normans and this was farmland then the park of a mansion until the late nineteenth century when these houses were thrown up. Two, we'll underpin the cellars and I've never heard of contiguous collapse of 'oles whatever the bloody hell that is. Three, we both know you ain't got no fucking insurance. I'll give you an extra two quid a truck and that's it.'

'You can't blame a fellow for trying,' he said, his straight-ahead eye smiling and twinkling with good-natured chagrin but the other one filming over with anger and disappointment.

'No, Sidney,' I said. 'I wouldn't have expected anything less from you.'

I'd left my bicycle at the bike park outside the station; when I rode into my own street it was twilight. Though I no longer drove I still noticed all distinctive cars around me and there was an unfamiliar black Mercedes CL 500 coupé with darkened windows parked a couple of doors up from my house. As I walked up the path to my own door, out of the corner of my eye I saw a man get out of the passenger side of the Mercedes and come towards me. Opening my front door slightly, giving me somewhere to escape to, I turned to face him. Suddenly running around in my head was the tune of an old club hit, 'Now That We've Found Love What Are We Going To Do With It?' by Heavy D and the Boyz. I waited for the man to reach me.

What I saw was someone of my own age, though racially what my old gran would have called 'half chat'. Small and lithe, dressed in a three-quarter-length black leather coat, narrow black trousers and a black roll-neck top not quite covering a chunky gold chain around his neck.

''Ello, Kelvin,' the man said.

''Ello, Machsi,' I replied.

'"Now That We've Found Love What Are We Going To

Do With It?" by Heavy D and the Boyz,' said Machsi Gorci.

'What?'

'What you're humming.'

'So it is. I didn't think I was doing it aloud. Those were the days, eh, back in the clubs?'

'Oh yeah,' said Machsi, middle son of the Gorci crime family. 'Hey, I'm glad you said "the days", 'cos I hate it when you see some fucking boyband cunts on MTV and they says, "back in the day". I mean what the fuck does that mean? "Back in the day"?'

'I'm fucked if I know, Machsi,' I replied. 'I particularly hate it when one of them bands refer to "their crew": I always think, What crew? Are you a fucking fishing smack or something?'

'Or how about "taking it back to the old skool". I always think Where? Like Eton or somewhere?'

'Das right.'

'Fucking right.'

After that there was an awkward pause so I said, 'Machsi, would you care to come in for an aperitif?'

'Naw thanks,' said Machsi. 'You know, I've got places to be, people to kill, that sort of thing.'

'Really? The last time I saw you, about eight years ago in Cream, you was loved up on E and you just wanted to stroke and hug everyone and be their friend for ever and not hurt them. What happened?'

'I read the government reports, man; that E's a dangerous fucking drug, it can do your head in.'

'Right. So now you're back in the family firm?'

'Das right.'

'Some aspect of which I imagine you wish to talk to me about.'

'Das right also. It's about that kid of your friend's.'

'Adam?'

'Correct.'

'What's the problem?'

'He's been dealing, coke and weed, buying from one of our local franchises. But been falling short on his payments – I assume he's been getting high on his own supply. Now in the normal run of best business practice I should have him severely beaten, but capricious acts of kindness being one of the perks of the job and as I'm aware of the trauma the lad's suffered with his dad getting killed and all that, I'm going to allow you to pay his debt instead, seeing as I know you care for the boy and you can afford it.'

'How much?'

'Nine hundred quid.'

'That's not particularly kind, after all you're getting paid.'

'But I'm diverging from what's expected, I'm still taking a risk. See, consistency is everything when you are dealing with people of low intelligence; they don't cope very well with nuance, and inevitably non-payment leads to a beating: that's clarity. Now however I introduce a variable, I let somebody else pay off this kid's debts, others will assume they can do the same so I'll need to be extra savage with them. Do you see, at the very least it means extra work for me and a small degree of danger, so don't tell me I'm not being kind.'

'You'll want cash I assume? I'll have somebody drop it off at your office tomorrow.'

'Cheers.' Machsi paused and said, 'Why aren't you frightened of me, Kelvin?'

'I dunno, it's odd isn't it?'

'Makes a pleasant change for me,' said Machsi Gorci as he turned and strutted back to his car.

A gaggle of teenage girls watched my every step with cold eyes as I walked up to the front door and rang the bell of the 1930s house in the leafy cul-de-sac where Paula and Adam lived.

Once inside I asked her, 'What is it with those girls?'

'They're hanging around hoping to catch a glimpse of Adam; if you'd been another girl they'd probably have attacked you.' She peered through the front window at the girls. 'That lot are the ones attracted to his doom-laden self-destruction; there's another gang that want to save him for Jesus: they sometimes have fights with each other.' Coming away from the window she reluctantly enquired, 'Do you want a coffee or something?'

'Yeah, that'd be great.'

I sat on the couch in her front room while she made it. I'd always been particularly fond of Paula, back in the day. Of all the girls in the group I'd got on with her the best; it had really upset me that I couldn't see her after the split with Colin. I suspected that she had had quite strong feelings for me too; there'd always been a little something extra between us. Before the accident I'd occasionally considered going round to her house one night, casually dropping in; in those days a lonely woman that knew me well was right up my street.

As she came back in carrying two coffee mugs I thought that she was still a very pretty woman, short and dark with olive skin, long auburn hair right down her back. She looked more like Adam's sister than his mum; in fact she didn't look like she had anything to do with him at all, which would have been a good thing since I suspected that boy was going to bring her a load of trouble.

'I wanted to talk to you about Adam,' I said.

'Oh fuck, what is it now?' she asked, her face going pale.

'He's been dealing drugs.'

'Shit!'

'Did you know?' I asked her.

'No. I mean I know he was smoking dope and stuff, all those losers he hangs with do that. Is it just dope he's selling?'

'No.'

'Oh, God. Are you certain about this – it isn't gossip or anything?'

'No and there's worse. Machsi Gorci came to see me. I had to give him nine hundred quid that Adam owed and couldn't pay.'

Now she was really frightened; she clutched her chest. 'Ah Christ, Machsi Gorci . . .'

'It's okay,' I said rapidly to calm her down. 'I paid him off. I paid him off and he'll make sure nobody'll give Adam credit no more, but he's been fucking stupid. Adam's going to get killed if he fucks around with the likes of Machsi Gorci.'

'I know. There was a kid in the next street that they dragged out of his gran's house and beat with baseball bats.'

I said, 'Do you want me to have a word with him?'

'I don't know what good that'll do,' she replied, twisting her fingers with agitation.

'Well, we get on, he might listen.'

'I guess,' she said without conviction. Paula called to her son. A few minutes later he came down the stairs and dropped on to the couch in the living room.

'Awright, Kelvin mate,' he said.

'Hi, Adam,' I replied.

'I'm not Adam no more,' he said. 'I'm DJ Rock.'

'Uh, okay.'

Before the trouble in the pub Adam's accent had been half Lancashire and half Liverpool; now he was talking in the intonations of an out-and-out Scouse scally. Also his clothes had changed: now he was wearing a shell suit composed of every pastel shade that there was. I was surprised to see that there was a pastel shade of black.

I tried to tell him in serious tones about my visit from Machsi Gorci. I might as well have been talking to my dad's dog – the boy didn't seem surprised or upset.

'Honest, mate,' he said, 'I'm sorry you was bothered. I'll pay you back, starting next week. Me and me mate Simon are making a record next week that's gonna be massive in the clubs. Then I'm going to Preston to do a three-year course in aeronautical design. An' you don't have to worry about the drugs – I've stopped doing that. I know I fucked up, Kelvin, Mum, but I'm gonna be clean and serene from now on.'

'Oh, Adam . . . er . . . DJ Rock,' his mum said, seeming really relieved, 'that's great, I'm so pleased.'

Not so easily placated, I enquired, 'This college, don't you need like science A levels?'

'You'd think so,' Adam said, 'but not if you show exceptional promise. I've done all these sketches of futuristic planes that they say are the best they've ever seen.'

I could see that might work for art school like it had done for me, but I was surprised that you could get on to an aeronautical design course that way; however there was no denying the kid's absolute sincerity so I guessed it must be so.

'Great,' I said.

'I could pay you back by direct debit,' the boy said. 'I'll set it up tomorrow.'

'Great,' I said again, though he never did.

When I got home from Paula's house it was eleven o'clock at night and Florence's truck was parked outside, bringing a sinister whiff of Balkan mountainside to this prosperous lane. That week cirKuss were in St Helens so it was only a twenty-five-minute drive for her.

In the month since we'd got together me and Florence had evolved a routine. Every week or every two weeks she would be performing in a different town in the north-west; if she was nearby, a couple of nights I would take taxis to where she was performing – sometimes I felt I'd run away from home to be *next* to the circus. After the show we might go out in the town or I would simply sleep over in her truck following a meal with the rest of the cast. I was often woken in the middle of the night by trouble, either between the cirKuss folk or the police being called or some irate father yelling about his dishonoured daughter.

Though the cirKuss performers generally had nothing to do with the ordinary inhabitants of the towns they visited, backstage there would sometimes be a local, generally a dusty-looking middle-aged man. One time in Bolton I asked one of them, 'What do you do?'

'I own a psychic shop,' he replied.

In Stockport I asked a similar-looking guy the same question and he said, 'I own a psychic shop.'

The cirKuss's day off was a Monday so after the show on Sunday night Florence would drive over to my place in her truck and we could play house till Tuesday afternoon with her in the role of the suburban English girlfriend. First thing on a Monday morning she would shake me awake, coerce me up and dragoon me into a forced march to the Safeway Superstore even if we didn't need any groceries. Ideally for her we would have gone there in some sort of small hatchback but I still wouldn't drive and her truck was too big for our tiny town centre, knocking over road signs and flattening parking meters the one time we tried it.

In the aisles of the supermarket she would make up stuff about our imaginary suburban life together. 'Oh, I think these eggs will be ideal for the omelettes I will make when your boss and his black mistress come for dinner,' she would say in a loud voice, or 'I need to buy home pregnancy kit for our daughter Flinka, where would I find that?' After shopping we would have the all-day breakfast in the Café Fresco that was attached to Safeway's.

One day when we were in there I said to Florence, 'I've been thinking I might throw a dinner party for a couple of friends of mine.'

'Yes of course,' she said in her loud voice. 'We will ask the Stampsons, Rabbi Kroll and his wife and maybe Captain Archer and some of the other female pilots from the airbase.'

'No,' I said, 'these people are actually really real; it's a guy called Sidney Maxton-Brown and his wife.'

'I suppose that would work too,' she answered.

The date was set for the next Monday night. When she thought about it Florence stated that she was very excited at the idea of this domestic activity, hosting a suburban dinner party, except she said she didn't want to do any shopping or cooking. I did all that.

* * *

A few minutes before Sidney and his wife arrived my home phone had rung. 'Hello?' I said. There was a hissing silence on the other end. 'Hello?' I asked again.

A heavily accented voice croaked, 'Stay away from her . . . you really stay away from her . . .'

'Valery?' I enquired, but the other end of the line had already gone dead.

Oh fucking great, I thought. A fucking big strong clown who's jealous of me and Florence is now bugging me on the phone, but putting the handset down I actually felt a bit pleased that Valery was so annoyed about us that he was moved to make threatening phone calls. It was a similar guilty little thrill to the one I experienced when men ogled Florence in bars and at the supermarket.

Before the accident, if I got bored during the day, sometimes I'd drive to the college where Siggi worked and slip into one of the media studies lectures she gave. They weren't hard to follow or anything since they seemed to consist mainly of watching ancient films and old telly programmes from the 1960s then talking crap about them. Back then, forty years ago, there used to be this thing called a *Wednesday Play* that they made everybody in the country watch because there was nothing else on the TV. A great number of these plays they transmitted appeared, from the ones we saw in the lectures, to be set at dinner parties, where these over-excited couples, who seemed to always work in something called 'publishing', would get drunk and bicker with each other and say terrible things and hold terrible secrets and throw stuff about and then events would end anticlimactically. My dinner with Sidney was a bit like that. I wondered if it made any difference in the old days, the telly being all plays about bickering publishers and discussion programmes with bishops, compared with the terrible fake reality shite we watch now. I don't suppose it did. I mean look at them places like where Florence comes from: the only thing they had on their TV was the ballet and folk singing yet they were still at each others' throats the first chance they got.

The Maxton-Browns arrived in a taxi right on 7.30, the exact time when they had been invited. Sidney was wearing black trousers with pockets high up on the legs stuffed with junk, overflowing with grimy handkerchiefs and big bunches of keys so that they increased the width of his already wide hips; as a top he wore a clinging green nylon roll-necked jumper that rippled over his corpulent body so that it not only emphasised his prominent man breasts but was so clingy that it made him appear as if he had man breasts on his back as well.

Sidney had brought a large plastic torch as a gift. Thrusting it at me he said, 'I don't know nothing about wine so I brung this . . . the batteries are inside. I knew you had to bring summat but I ain't never been to a dinner party before.'

'Well, that's very kind of you.'

'You know we don't actually have any friends whose houses we'd visit like, well we didn't before you come along . . . Barbara and me don't, you know, really mix with anybody outside the family so . . . My dad always says a friend is just a stranger who hasn't done you over yet. I bet you have loads of friends don't you, Kelvin? You seem the type, popular, well off.'

'Oh, friends, yes, lots of friends,' I said, 'but I've got space for a few new ones at the moment.'

Ushering them into the living room they sat perched on

the edge of my Atalanta couch. 'Can I get you some drinks?' I enquired.

'What do you recommend?' asked Barbara like I was a wine waiter at a Brewers Fayre Restaurant.

'They say a white wine is always nice,' I replied.

'That would be lovely then, thank you,' she said primly.

'The same for me, thank you,' said Sidney.

As I brought the drinks in I said, 'So, Sidney, you say you don't know anybody but family. I assume Barbara isn't family?' But then I thought maybe she was.

'Oh no,' said Sidney, smiling. 'It's a romantic story how we met. You remember those two lads, Venables and the other one who killed that Jamie Bulger kiddie? Well, one day I was down at the court when they was being tried, shouting and throwing eggs at the van they was in as they went into the court, you know, and Barbara happened to be next to me with a banner she'd made and we got chatting about how we hated people who hurt little kiddies and such, and one thing led to another . . .'

'That is romantic,' I said. 'Don't you think, though, that Venables and the other one were themselves just k—'

At that opportune moment Florence appeared wearing a short, low-cut, black dress. With one hand she was juggling three red peppers from the kitchen while the other held a tennis racquet with no strings that she'd found in the garage. Without stopping juggling she passed the raquet over her head and wriggled through it; as it travelled over her chest it nearly pulled one breast out of her dress.

Finally she stepped out of the racquet, caught all three peppers and gave an elaborate bow. Everybody clapped.

'I really like juggling, it's my favourite thing,' said Florence, smiling happily.

'Why can't you juggle?' Sidney said with some asperity to his wife. Then he said to me, easily loud enough for Barbara to hear, 'Fooking hell, she's a looker your girlfriend. Fooking hell she is.'

I was the one who did the cooking. As we ate I said to the two Maxton-Browns, 'See, Barbara, the meal you cooked me was great, all different stuff sort of fighting with each other, but you know there's a lot to be said for local produce and for restraint in cooking. What I've done is I've done us a vegetable soup made with produce bought from pensioners' allotments, no chemicals, see? Lancashire free-range organic pork from a farming cooperative near Burscough and apple pie from local apples, with Lancashire Tasty cheese under the crust, which I'm sure you know, Barbara, is a local recipe, topped off with ice cream from the farm shop.'

'Do you hear that, Barbara?' said Sidney Maxton-Brown. 'I want nothin' but organic local thingummy from now on. Then you might look a bit more like Florence.'

We sat down to eat. One of the things about Florence, she hated eating with cutlery, she said it was too heavy; the first time I'd cooked for her I'd put out my prized David Mellor cutlery, and she'd groaned when she saw it, then wearily lifted a fork as if it were made of atomically compacted vanadium. After a few minutes she'd thrown it down on to the table shouting, 'Ach, I can't eat with this, it's too fucking heavy!' So now while the rest of us ate with stylish pewter designer knives and forks, she consumed her entire meal from beginning to end with a tiny silver salt spoon. I thought it was one of the cutest things I'd ever seen but at one point Mrs Maxton-Brown nodded in Florence's direction and whispered something to her husband.

'I don't know,' he said.

She added another few words.

'No,' he hissed, 'I don't think she's got weak wrists from all her juggling.'

'Wow, Kelvin,' said Sidney, starting on his second bottle of my Gewürztraminer, 'that meal was really first rate. We're going to eat like that from now on definitely; you're not left with that chemical taste that you get in your mouth when you eat one of Barbara's meals.'

Then Sidney told us why he didn't like the Freemasons for thirty minutes, because apparently they had everything fixed for themselves and there was this bloke he'd known whose brother had invented a formula for turning water into petrol but the Freemasons had murdered him and destroyed the formula. Then he asked Florence if she wore pants and if she'd like to do some acrobatics for him, which was the point when Sidney's wife quietly began crying but he hardly noticed.

As he was standing on the step about to get into the waiting taxi with Barbara already inside, arms crossed over her chest, a sour expression on her face, Sidney suddenly said, 'Kelvin, can I have a quick word?'

'Sure,' I replied. 'What is it?'

'Something weird's been happening.'

'Oh yeah?'

'One of the nephews who's been driving for me told me, so I went with him to look for myself.'

'Yeah?'

'You know I told you we were going to fly tip some of your rubble?'

'I remember.'

'Well, the nephews dumped the first load like we agreed . . .'

I noted his attempt to implicate me in his dishonesty but didn't interrupt.

'. . . but when they got back the next day with the second load, it was gone.'

'What was gone?'

'The rubble, your, our rubble. Somebody's came in the night and took it away.'

'What, like the authorities?'

'No, not the fookin' authorities, they never do nowt; no, I reckon someone's stolen it.'

'That's mad, who'd want to steal rubble?' I said.

'I don't know! I don't know!' he squawked, suddenly agitated.

I said, 'Do you think somebody was so morally offended by the mess you made that they hired a truck and took it away themselves?'

With difficulty Sidney composed himself, though still with a worried expression he went on, 'I maybe just think some bastard has found a way to make money out of flytipped rubble and I can't figure out how. I tell you it's freaking me out. I don't mind if I know what's happening, I'll take on any foocker, it's the mystery I can't stand.'

'So what are you going to do?'

'I'm not going to fly tip no more, I'll tell you that. I'll pay the landfill fees before I let some other fucker at my rubble. Do you think there's a rubble-powered car? No, that's ridiculous.'

'Sidney,' I said, 'I was wondering if some time in the future you wanted to come and see a play with me.'

'A play?'

'Yeah, you know I was saying about making money, how it's easy for me. Well, I give it away too, I sponsor all sorts of arts events.'

Momentarily distracted from the mystery of the vanishing rubble by an even stranger thing, he asked, 'What do you want to do that for?'

'I think it makes the world a better place.'

'That's mad. You don't know all the world, they're strangers. I bet if you had a family you wouldn't give your money away.'

'I do have a family. Parent, sister in New Zealand, cousins, hundreds of them, that I don't ever see. They can look after themselves. I'd rather sponsor the arts.'

'I can't understand that but I suppose I'll come and see your play since you ask me. Will Florence be there?'

'I'm sure she will.'

'I'll come then.'

As he was about to get into the taxi, a police car turned into the end of my road and slowly cruised past, both officers in the front seats staring hard at Sidney. He turned to me, a look of panic in his eyes. 'See, see! They're still following me!' Then he shouted at the police car which was slowly and deliberately turning around a few metres further on up my road, 'I'm getting a cab, look, I'm getting a fooking cab! Leave me alone!!!'

After they'd gone Florence said, 'What a nice man. I think his wife had good time too; a pity she wanted to go home early with headache . . .'

Do you remember when that ferry sank? I think it was called something like *The Price of Free Enterprise*. (Was it really called that? It seems a bit metaphorical.) Anyway they found that there were two male passengers that drowned who were living complete double lives who had wives and kids and houses both in England and Holland, plus there were two other men that drowned whose papers were totally fake and they still have no idea who they were. So if you do a rough calculation, on average every ferry has at least four men on it living secret lives, men taking trips without explanation, who were vague about their movements and who didn't answer their mobile phones but always rang you back; every plane had maybe two, every train three and every vehicle with me in it at least one because I had not told Florence anything about the thing involving Sidney. To myself I said I wanted to keep her uncontaminated by what I was doing, figuring that she had been through too much already in her short life. I might have meant it, though there was something about having a secret mission that brought out the boy spy in me. Likewise there was no way to let Paula or any of the other relatives in on what I was up to; they definitely wouldn't understand.

As I've said there were many nights at the theatre from which I had got nothing at all, yet I still had this strong feeling that if I just could find the right play there would be something about the elemental, timeless nature of humans performing in a darkened room for other humans that might begin to connect Sidney with the empathy I hoped lay just below his skin. After all, that time Siggi forgot her lines was a night at the theatre that was going to stay with me for ever so it could happen.

However, realising I needed specialist help in choosing the right play, after making a few phone calls and telling Florence I was going to a conference on new developments in concrete, I took the train down to London. Not having taken an intercity train for years, I could see why people preferred to drive. Okay, in first class on the train they did come round with a trolley every five minutes offering you free stuff: sandwiches, booze, tortilla wraps, naanwiches, but there was a guy down the other end of the carriage listening to music on an MP3 player so loud it sounded as if his brains were being fried, every five seconds some idiot would get a call on their phone and three times the woman opposite me asked the trolley guy if he had a tomato but he didn't.

Since my unhappy year at college I had hardly visited London. My attitude to the place was a kind of defensive 'Who needs it?' type of stance. We had said to each other it was big and dirty and smelly, yet as I walked out from Euston into the arid little park where packs of drug addicts scurried away from the station in their stiff-legged, purposeful gait as if a commuter train had recently got in from Junkietown I suddenly understood why people said they liked the anonymity of the place. There was nobody in this gigantic city who knew me, I could be whoever I chose to be – now all I needed to do was think of somebody.

Walking south across central London through the university district and then the hi-fi and furniture shop district to my meeting, almost every road I tried to get down was blocked either by unattended flimsy plastic barriers, abandoned muddy, litter-filled trenches, stalled immobile cranes or roped-off mysterious piles of gravel in the middle of the pavement: whoever was responsible for all this disruption must have experienced a loss on the size of genocide to be digging up London on such a scale.

In the years since we had last met, on the day that Siggi had forgotten her lines, things had gone very well for Laurence Djaboff and then they had gone very, very badly. I'd followed his trajectory in the movie magazines that I read, the usual story of being lured to Hollywood, then of slowly being stripped of every precious principle and scruple and of being returned a broken and humiliated man. Now he was back in London and looking to return to the theatre, which wasn't proving as easy as he'd hoped, having made far too many enemies in that small introverted world.

We'd arranged to meet in one of those members-only clubs that they have in London so people in the entertainment business don't have to have anything to do with the public. Like some of the supermarkets I'd passed the club had its own beggar outside: sitting with his knees drawn up under a dirty pink blanket, he pleaded with me, looking up from the pavement with sad eyes, 'Got any spare change, mate?'

'No,' I said, 'but I'm always looking for workers in my business. I could give you my business number and guarantee you a good wage, maybe a place to stay, really get you back on your feet.'

From under his blanket came the James Bond theme rendered in tinny electronic tones; he fumbled about trying to smother it.

'Have you got a mobile phone under there?' I asked.

'Just fuck off will you, mate?' he said.

I always offered beggars a job when they tried to tap me for cash – I'd never met one yet who took me up on my offer.

Inside, the club was like one of those Escher prints, all narrow staircases that seemed to join up with each other so that you were going down when you thought you were going up. I gave my name to a slender French girl with a clipboard. Looking her up and down, I thought, My girlfriend's ten times better looking than you. After asking what my name was four times she told me Laurence was in the Reading Room. Shouting Room would have been a better name. The bar, all squeaky leather couches and hunting prints, reminded me of the ancient souk in Damascus; everybody seemed to be trying to sell something to the person they were with, frantically pulling ideas out of the air and yelling them at their companions.

He was sitting with a nearly finished drink in front of him. On this ordinary day Laurence Djaboff was dressed in a one-piece olive-green cotton jumpsuit like a tank commander might wear, thigh-high leather boots, a sleeveless untreated woollen waistcoat that smelled like a hot camel and a brown suede baseball cap worn backwards over his thinning grey hair.

After we'd ordered more drinks from a waiter I said, 'Your agent made it pretty hard for me to meet you.'

'Yes, sorry about that,' he replied, 'but you know I've had a lot of nutters pursuing me over the years. Presumably you'd be suspicious of an actor who came along and said he wanted to build some houses. So some builder no matter how successful wanting to finance a theatre tour . . .'

'I know,' I answered, 'but like I said to your agent, it will be in the nature of a memorial.'

'To Siggi who used to be in my company?'

'That's right.'

'I do remember her,' said Laurence wistfully. 'Terrific little actress, wouldn't sleep with me, she kept laughing on stage. Was that it? Was that why she left?'

'No. She forgot her lines and made some other ones up. In Liverpool.'

'Right. Ah, they go mad in so many ways: suddenly think

they can't act, get panic attacks, develop obsessions with their thumbs . . . and she was killed in a car crash?'

'That's right.'

'And you want to sponsor some shows of mine? Anonymously?'

'Yes, anonymously. Look,' I said, 'I've recently made a lot of money, have always been interested in the arts and you're the only actor I know. I read in the paper that you want to get back touring and thought I might be able to finance your tour. I mean since you set fire to the Arts Council headquarters there's not going to be any government—'

'Well, I'd signed a seven-year contract with NBC at the time, didn't think I was coming back to this stinking country. I didn't know they deported you from the States for low ratings.'

'Here's the thing,' I said, aware that I'd suddenly started talking like a character in a David Mamet play, 'here's the thing. What I want you to do is not put on one of your own plays, though obviously they're all great obviously. What I want you to do is this, to think of the most amazing play you ever saw in your life, the play that really changed you: I want you to stage that.'

As soon as I got back from the bar with more drinks Laurence Djaboff, who'd been deep in thought for many minutes, said, 'I know what it is!'

'Yes?' I enquired eagerly, sitting forward in my armchair.

'I doubt you will ever have heard of it, an early Howard Brenton play by the name of *Christie in Love*. Now you're too young to be aware but there was a time in the late sixties and early seventies when playwrights ruled the earth. Oh, it was the very heaven to be in the theatre then. Arnold Wesker had his own shop where you could buy all manner of Arnold Wesker products, and his chain of Chips with Everything restaurants. Snoo Wilson had four chart-topping number ones and was on a special Christmas *Top of the Pops* presented by Harold Pinter that was only eight minutes long and spoken in an entirely made-up language.'

I was pretty sure Laurence was making up all this stuff about the playwrights. We'd done *Chips with Everything* at school for A level English and nobody had mentioned the playwright owning a string of restaurants. Still, I didn't want to interrupt the flow.

'Now, it just happens at the moment to be the fashion in the theatre to revive plays from that period. Audiences watch them now in a completely different way, of course, for their strangeness. I imagine a lot of theatre-goers find early Dusty Hughes as difficult to understand as Chaucer. Okay now, this Howard Brenton play, I remember I went to see it at the Incendiary Device Theatre that used to be in Regent Street that only operated at lunchtimes; you could take your sandwiches in and eat them while you watched a play. Anyway, everything Howard Brenton has written before and since is complete shit but somehow in that one play, *Christie in Love . . .*'

Up until this point I had been sitting with a ridiculously dressed, mildly drunk little man, but as Laurence Djaboff began to describe the play, in some way he contrived to paint that autumn evening in late 1969 so vividly that it hung in the wine-stained, shout-filled air in front of my leather armchair.

'It was performed in the round like a lot of stuff was then, the set was wonderfully simple, a sort of pen about three metres by two and about a metre high made out of chicken wire full almost to the brim with torn-up and twisted shreds of newspapers. A claustrophobic atmosphere, very little space between the audience and the chicken wire, just enough room for the actors to walk around.

'As the public filed in with the house lights still on there was already a policeman digging with his spade into the newspaper like he was turning over a garden; before the play began he'd covered every inch of the pen. On the crappy old sound system over and over a tape broadcast details of Christie's life and of the women he had murdered. I'd bought a Dutch buckwheat pancake from a food cooperative to eat and as I bit into it the policeman looked straight at me, the house lights snapped off and he started to recite these filthy limericks: sickening they were. You see what the set represented was the garden of 10 Rillington Place where Christie had murdered and buried all these women and I remember at one point – it was the creepiest thing I've ever seen – Christie suddenly rose on a wire out of all the newspaper and he was wearing this horrible crude papier-mâché mask; it seemed impossible for anybody to be under all that paper, the policeman had walked and dug over every inch of it. It was the most extraordinary piece of pure theatre.

'It turned my head over, that play, because in its own way it was revolutionary; revolutionary for the time because part of the point of it was how terrible it was to be a copper, to encounter such awfulness and this was at a time when authority figures, coppers, soldiers, civil servants, were hated and despised by anyone on the left; we couldn't see them as human, we couldn't imagine that they had any feelings.'

'Laurence,' I said, 'that sounds exactly what I want.'

'We'll play small arts centres,' said Laurence, now in

full flow, 'maybe the odd derelict warehouse – that's very fashionable.'

'Oh, I can help you out there,' I said enthusiastically, then paused. 'There's only one other thing.'

'What is it?' he asked suspiciously.

'No, nothing to worry about. Only when the play gets to the north, when I come to see it there'll be a man sitting next to me in the audience. I want you to direct the whole play at him.'

A few hours later after many more drinks the whole thing was planned. I would provide twenty thousand pounds: this would buy me a tour of provincial arts centres and a possible London première at a theatre pub. My money would pay for a big van that the cast of three and two technicians and the set that the cast would put up would travel in. Laurence was going both to direct and star as the older policeman, the inspector. All in all it was a pretty good deal; that sort of money would only buy you shutting down Bury town centre for a fortnight at most.

My intention had been to take the afternoon train back to Liverpool from Euston but the evening found me still at the drinking club. At some point Laurence said to me, 'Old man, do you think you could lend me three hundred pounds?'

'Sure,' I said, drunkenly fumbling for my wallet (developers always carried plenty of cash). 'I didn't think you were so hard up that—'

'No, no!' protested Laurence. 'It's just I need the cash right now. I've had a few drinks and when I've had a few drinks that often makes me want to go and . . .' He paused.

Here we go, I thought, coke, prostitutes, boys, girls. Here's the problem.

'Makes me want . . . makes me want to go and buy a yo-yo.'

'A yo-yo?' I squawked.

'Yes, a yo-yo. I'm a big collector of yo-yos. There's a lot more to yo-yos than you think; you think they're just a fucking toy but you're a cunt if you think that. I bet you don't know this but the yo-yo was once a mighty weapon. A sort of oriental boomerang, a skilled hunter could bring down a flying bat with a well-aimed yo-yo. Then there were the bigger spiked war yo-yos of the Tang and Ming dynasty . . .'

So after a trip on two buses and the Docklands Light Railway, I found myself in a council flat in a place called Mudchute where an old man was unwrapping a selection of bejewelled and gold-plated yo-yos while a Chinese woman served us glass after glass of clear oriental spirit.

'I think you'll like this one, Mr D,' the old man said.

'Only silver plated but the string is pure silk with a lovely balanced action.' And a little while later as we walked through a council estate a couple of teenagers tried to mug us but Laurence knocked them both out with the yo-yo that he'd bought.

7

She pulled me through the bushes, leaves and branches slapping me in the face and getting in my mouth till we came out on the other side; now we were on the pavement of the A road that ran alongside the cirKuss campsite.

'See,' she said, pointing to a grey speed camera which was sited right by where we had emerged. Then she said, 'Watch this,' and quick as a squirrel climbed on to the top of the camera and squatted there, folding her limbs over in impossible ways and making herself very small. 'Get back in the bushes,' she hissed, so I retreated into the foliage, crouched under a laurel bush and watched and waited. A couple of cars sped past driving slightly over the limit but not quite fast enough to trigger the camera, then finally an old Montego appeared puffing along the road obviously sticking exactly to the 40 miles an hour limit. As soon as the car passed her Florence took out the two disposable pocket cameras that she'd bought in the petrol station earlier and one after the other let them off as the car passed, so that there was a double flash exactly as if the speed camera had been tripped. Florence quickly pocketed the cameras and slid sinously down the pole of the speed trap as the Montego fishtailed to a stop in a cloud of tyre smoke, and as the driver, a fat man in his fifties, came running back to the camera she slithered alongside me in the humid undergrowth and lay there racked with silent laughter.

'What the fuck are you talking about,' the driver shouted at the one-eyed metal troll that squatted by the roadside. 'I was fucking doing forty! That's the fucking limit, I was doing the fucking limit. What did you take my fucking picture for?'

Lying there laughing and laughing, I slid my hand down the back of Florence's jeans, slipped my fingers inside her pants and began stroking her between her legs. We got up and ran back, crouching low through the bushes, to her van. On the couch quickly she undid her jeans and I pulled them off, then I turned Florence over and slid myself into her from behind.

This time as I came my orgasm was accompanied by the sound of an old Montego reversing into a traffic camera at high speed.

Later, inside the van, we lay in her bed as thin autumn rain drifted on to the roof. Though my body was relaxed and spent, my mind was working late at the office; the problem was that I longed to know more about her. It made me uneasy that I still possessed only the faintest idea of the things in her past that had formed her and she rarely added to the scanty pile of information I held. It was only in moments of complete satiation such as this when her muscles slackened into my softer flesh and her breath stirred the few hairs on my chest that I was able to ask her carefully crafted pre-prepared questions designed to elicit precious biographical details.

Casually I queried, 'Florence, do you, you know, think people can change?'

Oh yes,' she said. 'I do, definitely.'

'Really?'

'Oh sure. You know I think it is one of the most amazing things about humans that there always seem to be some person, somewhere, who wants to do every single job that needs doing. Don't you think it amazing that there are always more or less enough men and women who really, really want to be undertakers, or cleaners of suicides off railway tracks, or bicycle messengers, or technicians who shove little TV cameras up old people's bottoms in the hospitals?'

'Right, I guess . . .' I said. 'So?'

'Okay. So you know those dolls they sell to the tourists in Russia?'

'Yes.'

'My country is like that, a country inside another country inside another country which is inside yet another country. This make everybody want to fight with everybody. So civil war breaks out once communists go and quick as porridge many people are ready and willing to consider a mid-life change of career, really happy to change. They suddenly eager not to be teachers or greengrocers or small farmers or technicians who shove little TV cameras up old people's bottoms any more but they want to be torturers, rapists, black marketeers, DJs who call for genocide over the radio, snipers hidden in the rubble and waiting patiently for days until the right little girl comes along to get water from the one standpipe; they turn out to be really good at it. And there even seem to be just exactly the right number of people who are eager to offer themselves as victims of the torturers and the snipers and the rapists by making defiant stand in the market place or sending their little girl to get water from the one standpipe or hiding people of the wrong religion in their lofts. So people can change, definitely yes.'

I felt awestruck to be in her presence like I imagined somebody might be on meeting Gandhi, though I doubted if their feelings of awe would be mixed with a desire to flip Gandhi on to his stomach and take him again right there and then, as mine were. That she could have been a victim of such things and still remain so lovely was amazing to me.

Then she said, 'I had a husband once . . . I think he died. But, darling, I cannot talk any more about it right now. When the time is right, then I tell.'

Leaving her truck in the early morning, a low mist lapped at my ankles as I searched for the key to unlock my bike; sensing a presence behind me I turned and saw Valery standing hunched in the lee of one of the wagons, his jacket wet with dew, staring hard at me. 'Don't marry her, you will be killed,' he called to me softly. I fumbled with the lock, jumped on my bike and rode away. 'You will be killed,' I heard again.

Laurence Djaboff had told me the quickest he could have the play *Christie in Love* ready to begin its national tour would be a couple of months. Until it was ready I had plenty of time to introduce Sidney Maxton-Brown to the concept of empathy to give him an inkling of how another human being felt.

And yet despite using a great deal of my energy I had no success at all in getting him to read books, attend concerts or go to art exhibitions; even if I said Florence was coming along he remained remarkably stubborn and simply refused to go. The one thing he would do was watch films with me, so in the end I devised a curriculum of movies that I thought might go some way to elevating a person. Once or twice a week I got him to come round to my house to watch movies. Many nights Sidney and me and Florence would sit in front of the plasma screen watching *Broadcast News*, the entire canon of Laurel and Hardy and the Marx Brothers, Almodóvar's *Live Flesh* but none of his other films, *ET*, the original *Rollerball*, Peter Yates's *Breaking Away*, Karel Reisz's *The Gambler*, Paul Verhoven's *Robocop* and *Starship Troopers*, the complete works of Eisenstein, Buñuel and Billy Wilder.

Sidney certainly enjoyed himself immensely but I didn't really sense that these masterpieces of the cinema were causing any noticeable increase in his empathy. There was, though, something else that did really seem to be unsettling him and that was friendship itself. Sidney told me after he'd sat blithely smiling through Pier Paolo Pasolini's *Theorem* that the day before he'd informed the many members of his family to universal astonishment that he had a friend and that he went places with his friend. He said they couldn't see the sense in it.

Having a friend didn't seem to make him happy either. He took to phoning me six or seven times a day to ask anxiously what I was doing and did I know what Florence might be doing, and he was constantly demanding guidance on how he should behave in front of people: what sort of a fork should you eat avocados with? Was it bad manners to take an Alsatian dog to a wedding? Should you tip a rabbi?

The police still kept a close watch over Sidney: a couple of crackheads who grabbed the money he'd just taken out of an ATM machine in the town centre were astonished that four officers were on them before they had got five feet, but by and large he seemed to have got used to it.

One night early in November I slept over in Florence's truck.

The next morning when I got back to my house there was a message from Paula on the answerphone. 'Kelvin,' I heard her say in a tight voice, 'can you come round? I need to talk to you urgently.'

Oh fuck, I thought.

'It's Adam,' she said as I seated myself in her living room.

'I guessed as much. He never set up that direct debit you know.'

'Yes, yes. I'll get you the fucking money,' she retorted impatiently.

'I wasn't saying . . .' I gave up. 'So what's wrong? Where is he?'

'He's upstairs. God, it's been awful. He's been doing like an enormous amount of cocaine and now he's become convinced that the fridge in the kitchen is trying to kill him.'

I couldn't help laughing at this. 'The fridge?'

'It's not funny, Kelvin.'

'Sorry, nerves.'

'Okay, I know it sounds stupid. People think coke's harmless but it can give you terrible paranoia. There's a lad in the next street who cut one hand off because he thought it was trying to take money out of his bank account. Adam's been cutting himself as well.'

'Cutting himself?'

'Slashing his arms with kitchen knives, burning his skin with cigarettes, all the fun of the fucking fair. He'll kill himself if he doesn't get help right away. The GP's been round and tranquillised him for about ten hours. Reason I called you, see, I've spoken to this addicts' treatment centre down south, a place called Muddy Farm. They say that they can take him in right away, it's only . . .'

'What?'

'It's three grand a week . . .'

'Jeez . . .' I said.

'I know.'

'Well, I guess I can pay that. I mean they'll cure him, right?'

'Oh, I'm sure they will, I mean that's what it's there for. These people know what they're doing and I promise I'll pay you back.'

'Don't worry, if it gets him better . . .'

'The other thing: can you, could you, drive us down there now?'

I felt a shiver of fear. I said, 'I haven't driven since the accident.'

'I know,' she said. 'I wouldn't ask you but I don't know anybody else or I . . .'

'Yeah, all right.' I didn't think it was true that she didn't know anybody else who could help her, at least with the driving part. I sensed even in the middle of her misery that it was a part of my punishment that she gave me these tasks. I actually felt no guilt, knew I wasn't obliged to help her but I did anyway. It came to me that I might as well use this opportunity as a way to get back in a car. I said, 'I think I'll be okay to do it.'

I left her house and walked the mile into town, to where there was an Avis office and rented a Ford Mondeo. I asked but they didn't have anything smarter like a Merc or something. When I looked I was surprised to find my driving licence was still in my wallet, though when they asked for it at the rental desk, taking it out the photo looked nothing like me. A youth delivered the car to the front door of the office with a screech of tyres, the girl behind the desk handed me the keys, I went outside, unlocked the door, climbed behind the wheel. Adjusting the seat and the mirrors, that took up a few minutes, waiting for the walls of the car to come in and crush me used up another five; when nothing happened, the ignition fired up like all the cars I'd ever driven, put it in gear and drove away from the kerb. What did I feel? There was certainly a greater vigilance in my mind. I knew driving would never be the forgetful, automatic activity it had once been; I had a vague sense that every car coming towards me was planning to veer into my path but it was nothing I couldn't cope with.

On returning to Paula's house we went upstairs together to get her son; the drugged bandaged boy was just about able to stumble down the stairs with me and his mother holding him under the arms. I opened the back door of the car and we tipped him in; he fell sideways and slumped insensible across the rear seat.

Late morning had arrived by the time we got going. With the low winter sun shining in my eyes I stuck to quiet country roads, easing myself in gently to the business of driving.

'Kelvin,' Paula said, 'we'll never get there at this rate. Get on the fucking motorway.'

As she spoke we passed a junction sign for the M6. I didn't give myself time to think about what was happening as I swerved up the slope, crested the rise, we rolled down the ramp and joined the deluge of traffic heading south. As I swung into the middle lane to overtake a truck a Skoda Fabia driven by a middle-aged woman went past me in the outside lane. I guessed she was doing at least 95 miles an hour. In the split second that we ran parallel I glimpsed all along the top of the car's dash she'd arranged fluffy animals and brightly coloured stuffed furry toys.

'That's better,' Paula said.

Somehow, despite its grim purpose, the drive turned into a happy excursion for the two of us. Sealed in that metal shell, stopping at motorway services, so that one of us could run in, use the toilet, grab a coffee and a pack of sandwiches trapped in a plastic triangle and run out again, we somehow lost the edginess that had been between us and became friends once more.

She said, 'You know the Friends and Family Group is campaigning for a memorial? Apparently, though, you have to have at least ten deaths before the authorities will even consider it. Wanna help with a petition?'

'I dunno, maybe,' I said. 'I'm sort of working on a memorial of my own.' Then in case I'd revealed too much enquired, 'Still leaving the flowers?'

'Yeah. Colin's brother says it'd be cheaper for us all to buy our own florists. And of course we can't stop on the hard shoulder to leave them at the site of the . . . so we have to park in a country lane and then walk across four fields, one with a bull in it and the farmer is starting to turn nasty. It's hard to know whether we're doing the right thing.'

I said, 'Yeah, I know what you mean. We're not used to coping with death any more. I mean our ancestors had tons of practice, people were pegging out all the time, half their children didn't survive to adolescence, pimples could be fatal in the Victorian age. And belief of course, they had that as well, the whole community knew what to do but . . . well, like Siggi's funeral that was particularly . . . awful . . . her friends from drama school singing "Wake Me Up Before

You Go-Go". I don't remember her ever saying that was her favourite song.'

Paula laughed. 'No, I think we're pretty much connoisseurs of funerals now and I have to say I reckon you're better off sticking with a straight Church of England in my opinion. Unless you're a Muslim or something.' Then she said suddenly, 'I've joined a road campaign organisation as well.'

'Well, that's good, isn't it?' I replied, wishing to keep on her good side now that we were mates again.

'I dunno, in a way, there's four thousand people killed on our roads every year and we just sort of put up with the situation; it's fucked up if you think about it. But you know I keep saying to myself, in a way it's selfish, you join this organisation because this thing has happened to you – but if I'd been a decent person I should have been in it already, I should have noticed all these people getting killed. I mean they do get mentioned in the papers: once you start looking, you see it all the time, whole families killed, groups of friends wiped out, children orphaned yet I did nothing. Like those people collecting in the pub to buy a scanner for the local hospital because their nephew's got leukaemia but they didn't give a fuck about leukaemia before somebody they knew got ill, did they? If they were really moral they would have cared about the scanner before. I should have cared without my husband being killed by that one-eyed bastard Sidney Maxton-Brown.'

Over the phone Paula had been told the treatment centre was just a mile and a half after you passed through a village called Poulsen in the county of Surrey. As we drove slowly through this place it seemed to contain an extraordinary number of pubs, wine bars, bodegas, hotels and off-licences: one after another they were strung out along the main road, their jaunty neon signs illuminating the black night.

Since turning off the motorway half an hour earlier no other inhabited place we'd been through had contained more than one gloomy pub or shuttered-up liquor shop but as we passed the post office in Poulsen I saw that even it had a big poster in the window offering twenty alcopops for five pounds. Initially unable to recall where the village of Poulsen reminded me of, I realised eventually it was a place we had visited on our holiday in LA: the Mexican border town of Tijuana.

Exactly a mile and a half further on by the car's trip computer there was a tiny wooden sign which read 'Muddy Farm' stuck in the grass at the mouth of a long, tree-lined, potholed drive. An iron gate hanging off one hinge was pushed back into the laurel bushes.

As I gingerly drove down the track we could see hunched figures in the darkness walking furiously up to the gateway puffing on cigarettes; when they got there they spun round angrily and stalked back.

At the end of the drive there was a long, low Queen Anne farmhouse, its doorway surrounded by coloured light bulbs which only served to make it seem even more mournful. On the broad gravel square in front of the house a number of Porsches, Jaguars, Audi TTs and an antique Bentley were parked all askew with tyres half flat, their expensive paintwork streaked with tree sap, bird droppings, twigs and leaves as if they had been stalled there for quite some time.

I put our rental car next to one of the Porsches whose sloping bonnet was half buried in a hedge and between me and Paula we managed to half drag, half carry Adam to the porch. We propped him against a wall, Paula unlatched the carved oak door, then again we both took an arm and carried the boy inside.

A cube of hot air hung inside the reception area of Muddy Farm; it reminded me of any number of the disappointing country house hotels that me and my mates had stayed in over the years gone by; linen-fold oak panelling halfway up the walls, an artificial ficus plant in the corner and a desk with a grease-smeared obscurely branded computer on it. Behind the desk sat an enormously fat woman dressed in what looked like a Mongolian yurt. She looked up as we dropped Adam like a bag of shopping into an armchair. 'Hello,' she said, smiling warmly, rose, steered her bulk round the desk, knocking some pencils on the floor, and came towards us holding out her hand. 'I'm Klinky Poon, senior counsellor. Welcome to Muddy Farm. I assume you're Paula and this is Adam, we've been expecting you.'

We all, except Adam, said hello.

'Now first of all let's get the formalities over with,' Klinky said. She went back and sat behind the desk. Drawing a form out from a filing cabinet she indicated we should sit at the two chairs facing her.

'Now first of all we have to get down a few details. Here at Muddy Farm in a supportive atmosphere of love and trust we try to shepherd the addict towards recovery and sobriety. So first of all does Adam have health insurance?'

'Er . . . no,' said Paula. 'My friend here, his godfather, Kelvin, is going to pay.'

'Right,' said Klinky, immediately picking up a phone and pressing an internal line, 'well in that case he should talk to our financial officer Akbar Akbar. Kelvin, you can use my desk, while us girls go into the lounge and get on with the pastoral stuff.' Then into the handset, 'Akbar, can you come to the front desk please.'

I was a bit surprised: you could understand nurses being on call round the clock but that there would be a financial officer available at nine thirty on a Tuesday night seemed a little mercenary. Then I dismissed the thought from my mind; I was sure these were good people.

While Paula gave details of Adam's health and his drug taking I filled out a cheque for six weeks' shepherding towards recovery and sobriety which came to eighteen thousand pounds, made payable to 'Monastery Group Health Facilities PLC'. I'd heard of the Monastery, it was a famous treatment centre in London; I hadn't known they owned Muddy Farm too. It was a lot like pubs where you thought you were drinking in some little country inn but when you looked at their sign it turned out to be owned by a giant corporation. I suppose when you thought about it pubs and Muddy Farm were in the same business.

From where I sat with Akbar emptying my current account I glimpsed, hidden out of sight from normal view under Klinky's desk, its maw gaping open to reveal its ravaged insides, the biggest bag of Fun Sized Bounty Bars that I'd ever seen.

Adam was then taken off to see a nurse to begin his detox while me and Paula were given a tour of the rest of the house. Up and down narrow stairs through plywood fire doors we went. We were shown the rooms where the addicts slept: again they reminded me of bed and breakfast hotels in provincial towns, except here there were six or eight beds squeezed into the space where there would normally only be a queen-sized double and a trouser press.

Klinky said that for the first week Adam would not be allowed to contact anybody outside. After that he could use the payphone in the cabin off the reception area.

She also showed us the lounge, the lecture room and the gym in the stables opposite: not very well equipped, it was like one I used to go to in the late eighties when a bench press seemed as miraculous a contrivance as a time travel machine. Klinky told us most of the addicts weren't allowed to use the gym anyway because if they couldn't get drink or drugs they'd become hooked on exercise.

There was a dining room where the patients were served three stodgy meals a day and Klinky said they had to sit at the table for at least half an hour because the food addicts ate very slowly, if they ate at all, and always under supervision because they either tried to steal the meals of others or attempted to hide their own dinners down the back of the sofa.

Back at reception Klinky, picking up the phone, her podgy fingers hovering over the numbers, told us they had an approved hotel in the village and would we like her to book us a room for the night? I told her no because I had to get back to Liverpool for the première of a play.

Notwithstanding that it was November the terraced houses all around Liverpool's football ground had draped themselves in bright Christmas lights that chased each other up and down the PVC double glazing and around the flimsy wooden front doors, plastic Santas and reindeer balanced insecurely on their satellite dishes rocking backwards and forwards in the wind pixilating the pictures on the TVs below. It was an idea they'd picked up from holidays in Florida, though it made their houses look more like Blackpool.

It seemed to be my week for walking through entrances draped with lights. Across the road the site entrance to Kelvinopolis – now named the Crystal Quarter by the estate agents who'd won the contract to pre-sell the apartments – was also adorned with lights. The rows of bulbs reminded me of Muddy Farm but also, with a familiar, though diminishing stab of memory, of the trip to see cirKuss with my friends in that prelapsarian time when the world seemed free of danger and doubt.

The decoration of the building site wasn't premature Christmas illumination but rather signalled the Liverpool première of Laurence Djaboff's startling new production of Howard Brenton's play *Christie in Love*; a production which had been drawing ecstatic reviews in every town it had so far played in. Ticket touts who usually worked six streets over around the gates of Anfield Football Ground were wheedling at the invited guests for spare tickets. In much the same way as my business had prospered through my inattention, so it seemed that my investment in the play, though made for ulterior motives, was also starting to turn a profit. Moreover, though my backing was supposed to be anonymous, word was already starting to spread in the arts world of a hot new impresario operating around the north-west: after all, they said, who would have thought of backing a played-out old cunt like Laurence Djaboff and inspiring him to do such remarkably good work?

More strings of light bulbs led the excited, twittering, first-night audience across duckboards to the pub, now hollowed out and waiting to be refitted with its smart new architect-designed interior. For the next two weeks the space would be arranged as a hundred-and-fifty-space theatre, the banked seating surrounding on all sides the chicken-wired set inside which the police constable was already in place, inexorably digging his way through the knee-deep, screwed-up newspaper.

Feeling like some provincial Irving Thalberg with the most beautiful girl in town on my arm, I stood at the entrance to the pub welcoming the long snaking line of my invited audience. Florence had taken the night off from the cirKuss and stood beside me, my consort, dressed in a grey Jill Sanders suit I'd bought her in Manchester.

It had been an effort at first getting a lot of the arts establishment of Liverpool here, but now that they were they felt a thrill go down their trousers when they saw that Machsi Gorci and most of his family were also present. The Gorcis sat imperiously looking about them as if they were at a boxing match, pleased to have stolen a march on the other crime families and to be getting their pictures in the papers for something other than murder and mayhem. The remaining crime families, seeing these photos the next day, assumed the Gorcis had found a new area to expand into, were getting some financial rake-off or tax write-down from the show and for a while after that touring plays, comedians and dance companies received sinister visits from frightening men. I'd had to do some lying in order to ensure that Paula and the other relatives were invited for another night as they couldn't be allowed to see the person I regarded as the guest of honour, Sidney Maxton-Brown, who was at that moment arriving at the site gate in an armoured personnel carrier bearing the markings of Zhukov's Soviet Sixth Guards Army.

'Where's Barbara?' I asked as he came towards me across the duckboards.

'Oh, I told her not to come, I said she wouldn't understand it or know anybody. Hello, Florence, blurry hell you look lovelier than ever.'

When he looked at my girlfriend like that, one good eye shining with naked lust while the other stared off into the corners of the world with a Noël Coward-like ennui, I had to repress a violent internal shudder. All the time I'd spent with Sidney had not made me like the man any more than I had the first time I'd met him. I reflected that my recent experience couldn't be one that many people had. Perhaps girls who worked for escort agencies would understand what I was going through, spending my time going to plays and watching films with somebody that I hated and despised. Except even the men those girls went out with hadn't killed five of their friends, so really the only escort girls who might understand something of what I was experiencing would be ones who'd spent a few evenings with the Yorkshire Ripper.

I showed Sidney to his reserved seat right on the front row, I sat on one side of him, Florence on the other. With childish eagerness he kept wriggling on the edge of his seat. 'I'm really looking forward to . . .' he said, but never got to finish as suddenly the constable's head spun round to fix Sidney with maniacal staring eyes, the house lights snapped out and the policeman pinned in a single cold spotlight began to speak his filthy limericks.

* * *

I had read enough biographies of Irving Berlin and Terence Rattigan to know that the impresario threw a glittering after-show party on the first night. Mine was held in a big tent across the other side of the site: I made a little speech and presented Laurence with a gold Louis XIV yo-yo, there was free champagne and the latest style of canapé – tiny sausages split with mashed potato piped into the slash, quails eggs with slivers of toast sticking out of them, mini Yorkshire puddings stuffed with beef and gravy.

Sidney had been strangely quiet during the interval and afterwards I'd been too busy receiving the congratulations of the many new friends I'd just made to find out what effect the play had had on him. When things got a bit quieter I went searching in the press and found him standing alone in a corner staring into his flute of flat champagne. I said to him, 'Hello, mate, are you all right?'

There was a pause, a sort of freezing you sometimes get when your satellite TV picture is hit by sunspots. Sidney looked up as if seeing someone he didn't know. 'Oh, hi, Kelvin . . . yeah, sure, fine. Where's Florence?'

'I think last time I saw her she was asking Machsi Gorci's mum why all her kids were different colours.'

'Right . . .' Then he said, his voice shaking a little, 'Blimey, Kelvin, I know I've never seen a play before but those three blokes have got to be fucking brilliant actors! Do you know I had this weird feeling that they were doing like their whole performance to me alone? As if they was doing it all just for me . . . I suppose everybody feels that. But they really got the play over. I mean I've always hated the police, well you would, yet I never realised before what it must be like being a copper: interviewing nonces, telling people their kids are dead, digging up bones at murder sites, going to all kinds of a—' Here he stopped.

'All kinds of what?' I asked.

'Accidents.'

'Yeah, accidents,' I said. 'They must see some terrible things, coppers, at all those accidents, people with their guts hanging out, heads stove in, squashed flat by trucks and that . . .'

'I'm sorry,' said Sidney, 'I feel a bit odd . . . something I . . . I think I'd better go home. Will you phone the nephew to bring the APC round the front?'

'Sure I will. Yeah, you go home,' I said.

'Will you ring me a couple of times tomorrow?'

'I'll look forward to it,' I replied, and for the first time in our relationship I meant what I said.

As promised, I called Sidney twice on the day following the première of *Christie in Love* and all through the week until I was free enough of business concerns and able to take the time off to go and visit. On the phone he wasn't able to be specific about what was upsetting him, indeed I doubt whether he quite knew what it was himself.

A concerned-looking Barbara Maxton-Brown was waiting on the verandah to greet me.

'Sidney's in bed,' she said. 'It's not like him. Now you're here I'll try and get him up.'

I went into the lounge and waited. Eventually Sidney emerged still in his pyjamas with a crumpled tartan dressing-gown badly tied around him.

In person Sidney was even less his former bumptious self; he had the air of a man who had been unexpectedly turfed off his charter plane into a vast and puzzling country, filled with sights and wonders but whose rituals and manners were entirely strange and unfamiliar.

'Hi, how you doing?' I asked.

'Oh, not too good,' replied Sidney in a weary, tentative voice. ''Ere,' he said.

'Yeah?'

'You know you told me to watch that QVC shopping channel because they had loads of great bargains on there?'

'Yeah, that's right.'

'Well, you didn't tell me it's fooking depressing; it seems to me a lot of those people on there, they're just buying stuff because they're lonely and they're desperate for somebody to talk to and the only ones they can think of to talk to is this fooking home shopping channel that's abusin' their misery. It's really upsetting me but somehow I can't stop watching and I can't stop buying Beanie Owls.'

'Hmm, is that so?' I said. 'Well, I'm sorry you're not feeling too good. What are you doing during the day?'

'I'm watching too much telly and it's all upsetting me; there was this couple on a home make-over TV show and they just couldn't find the right wallpaper and they got really upset about it and then I got really upset about it, then I started crying. It's stupid, isn't it, getting upset about wallpaper.'

'Do you think?' I said. 'I've wondered a lot about this and the thing is, we have no way to measure pain, do we? I sometimes think that maybe the rich lady who can't find the right handbag or whatever and she gets really distressed, maybe the amount of pain she's feeling to her it's the same as somebody who's . . . oh, I don't know, lost all their friends in some kind of accident. Do you think it's the same or do you think there's some quality to massive suffering that's different? What do you think, Sidney?'

'I don't know,' said Sidney, 'I don't know.'

I said, 'Well anyway, it's not good for you hanging around the house all day getting all lethargic, I think what you need is a little holiday. That'll perk you right up. So how about you and me take a little mini break to Amsterdam?'

I bought myself a car, a silver one. I couldn't recollect what make it was and often I'd forget where I'd left it in supermarket car parks. I didn't use it much but guessed it was handy to have around. Mostly it stayed parked outside my house.

In bed one night, Florence and I were talking when she suddenly said, 'You know when you get new mobile phone then the battery lasts maybe five, six days, how that make you feel?'

'It makes me feel like I can use my phone?'

'No, fool.' She laughed. 'It make you feel good. When your phone battery is strong you feel strong.'

And here I thought of what I hadn't thought of for days: the accident, how I'd imagined I could keep Loyd alive with my mobile phone. For such a long time they'd been a strong constant in the front of my mind and now they were getting indefinite and wispy like a faint fog, impossible to hold and grab on to.

Not noticing my absorption Florence went on, 'Now when you have your phone for a long time, maybe a year or two and you have to recharge it every day, how you feel then?'

'Bad?'

'That right! When your battery weak you feel weak, so what I think would be a great thing to have is a thing about size of small phone, small black box and you charge it up and it stay charged for long time like twenty days.'

'And what else does it do?'

'Nothing – it just stay charged so you feel charged, you feel strong.'

'Right,' I said.

'Well, I been thinking I might like to be an inventor when I get too crippling with arthritis to perform in the cirKuss and maybe I invent such a thing.'

I asked, 'Do you have arthritis?'

'No, now I got to go pee,' she said, sliding out of bed. I watched her exquisite back as she disappeared into the bathroom.

As if it knew we'd been talking about it my mobile phone, which was lying by the side of the bed, starting vibrating until it fell off the bedside table and on to the floor. Idly I picked it up. ''Ello?'

'Keep away from her,' a voice said.

'Hi, Valery,' I replied. 'How's it going?'

'You keep away or you die . . .'

'Yeah, yeah, this is getting old . . . goodbye.' And I broke the connection.

'Who was that?' she asked, wriggling back under the sheets and rubbing herself against me.

'Just business,' I said.

It rained a lot in early December, soaking the thick black soil to the consistency of Christmas pudding. I could really have done without taking a trip to the Netherlands but I wanted to capitalise on Sidney's wobbly state so I cleared some space in my busy developer/arts entrepreneur schedule. Even so, in the end our trip would have to be midweek because one of the few things I couldn't cancel was my first visit to Adam at the addiction treatment centre in Surrey.

The boy had been at Muddy Farm for five weeks and they were talking about letting him out after seven or, to put it another way, after twenty-one thousand pounds.

Paula had already made a couple of visits by train and taxi which she said had taken most of a day. Even driving it, when there wasn't an emergency, was such an undertaking that me and Paula decided we would travel down on the Saturday morning and stay overnight at one of the many hotels in Poulsen, in rooms that were done in a similar chintzy style to the treatment centre except that they only had one bed in them. Then we would drive back to the north on the Sunday night after the final compulsory group interaction, hopefully late enough to avoid the traffic round London.

It was one of those rare mornings when only the good drivers seem to be out, no fucking trucks, no ten up Bangladeshi families in two-hundred-year-old Toyotas, no old geezers dreaming up the middle lane in a permanent vegetative state. Just the big silver German sports saloons riding low on their springs snicking in and out of the inside lane at 99 miles an hour, blipping their lights to move you over and flashing thank you with the hazards. So we reached the village of Poulsen earlier than planned, about lunchtime. No point in hanging around: we dropped our bags at the hotel and drove straight on to Muddy Farm.

There were many more cars parked outside the house than there had been when I'd taken Adam there originally so I was forced to leave mine further down the potholed drive and walk back. All around, other weekend visitors were drifting towards the farmhouse; they had the same concerned, absorbed look on their faces as I'd seen on those attending an avant-garde performance art event. Behind me as I was locking the car, two matching black BMW X5 four-wheel drives pulled up with a crackle of gravel. A smartly dressed young man got out of each, blipped their locks and headed briskly towards the house: to me they looked like the most obvious drug dealers I'd ever seen.

'Welcome to Alcotraz,' said Adam with a twisted smile when we met him in the reception area.

Though I tried to hide my feelings the boy's appearance was shocking. There were a number of large sores on his lips and forehead, his hair was lank and greasy, one eye was filmed over and cloudy and when I hugged him I felt his bones, he seemed terribly thin. In contrast, the teenager's manner appeared extremely bright, overbright if anything, like a star about to burn out.

The drill at Muddy Farm was that we had a couple of hours of free time to chat uncomfortably with whichever addict we'd come to visit then at three o'clock prompt there was a compulsory group interaction: this was where all the patients and their guests sat in a big circle and talked about the wonderful world of addictions.

After a while I left Paula and Adam to talk and went outside to the silent, sodden trees at the rear of the house. Down a wood-chipped path I came to a bench by a large ornamental fish pond, the water of the pond entirely covered by a stout net, presumably to prevent the patients throwing themselves into it. At three I returned. The group interaction began with a reading of AA's twelve steps. Klinky had told us previously that Muddy Farm was a therapeutic community utilising the principles of Alcoholics Anonymous. When Adam had first gone completely off the rails, as is my way I'd read everything I could about AA. Knowing little about the organisation beforehand I had always thought of it as being a rather silly, mad, culty outfit but the more I read the more impressed I became. While some of the stuff about your God and your higher power seemed clunky and old-fashioned they still appeared to have found a way to navigate around all the problems that bedevilled every other group of individuals who got together for any purpose, from the smallest fishing club to the Politburo of the Communist Party of North Korea. They held no money so nobody could embezzle or abuse the funds; they took no position on anything and endorsed nothing so their principles could never be subverted by commercial sponsors; they had no permanent officials so no control freak was inclined to weasel their way into a position of power and they demanded total honesty from their members in all aspects of their lives. I had wondered briefly if I couldn't somehow convince Sidney Maxton-Brown that he was an alcoholic, even though mostly he only drank the odd glass of wine or beer, then lure him to some AA meetings.

It was a pity in a way that Alcoholics Anonymous had nobody to speak for it. I would have liked to ask them how they felt, as an organisation that had worked out all this great stuff and gave it away for free, about their method being used by a place like Muddy Farm that charged its inmates three grand a week.

In the lecture room we formed a circle sitting on hard chairs, the patients and their guests; it reminded me of the few art history seminars I'd gone to when I'd been at art school in London. As a matter of fact now I looked closely I saw that one of the patients was actually the rich girl from the art history seminar fifteen years ago, the one who'd gone on about her flat in Rome with the Van Gogh painting hanging in the hall, the one who'd made me feel so bad; now she was grown up or rather shrunk down into a wizened, stick-thin woman, with obviously false breasts protruding from an emaciated frame. Judging by what was said at the group meeting she'd spent the last few years whoring herself for crack cocaine so it wasn't true that she would never want to fuck me after all: if I'd bumped into her before her family had got her into Muddy Farm and I'd had a ten pound rock on me she would have done it no problem. The two drug dealers were her visitors; they sat either side as she reeled off a decade and a half of pain in her posh voice. It was not the woman's first time in a treatment centre; at one point she was saying, 'When I was in the Monastery for the second time, which was after I was in the Pledge Centre and Shadows but before my six months at Rippling Pines . . .' I figured, assuming those places cost roughly the same as Muddy Farm, that her family had spent maybe a hundred thousand pounds and, judging by what I saw, she was certainly nowhere near being fixed.

Most of the others in there were the same, having done time in many different places: it seemed that along with drugs, drink, sex, exercise, eating, vomiting, starving, cutting, they were also addicted to treatment centres.

I sort of had the idea that you went into one of these joints and they cured you; considering the amount of money they charged you would sort of expect it – that's what happened in the movies: you went into rehab and you got better. I thought if they were charging so much and yet nobody was getting fixed then wasn't it simply some sort of racket?

If these people were buildings, the trades and standards inspectors would be round in no time.

'I don't know about you,' I said to Paula as soon as we got back to the hotel, 'but I need a fucking drink!'

'Yeah,' she replied, laughing. 'And a line of coke and a needle full of heroin and some paint stripper.' Without bothering to go up to our rooms and change or anything we went straight to the flock-wallpapered bar and ordered two triple gin and tonics and a bottle of strong lager each. A few minutes later the parents of a pretty anorexic girl about Adam's age came in; they ordered quadruple Southern Comforts with ice. Seeing as we now knew every detail of the things their daughter did in the toilet it seemed only polite that we said hello to them and enquired whether they'd like to sit with us, which they did. In a short while a lot more of the relatives and friends had drifted by and soon we had a party going. The mother of a heroin-smoking merchant banker, who'd been sitting at our table crying, slipped off upstairs with the two guys from the black BMWs and came back twenty minutes later looking a lot more animated, the brother of an alcoholic airline pilot went out to get the CDs from his car and was soon blasting Moby over the hotel's feeble sound system and the girlfriend of a depressed and crack-addicted supermodel took her top off and danced wildly to the music on top of a table.

It was probably one of the best parties I've ever been to, sitting in a hotel lounge getting drunk and fucked up with a load of sad, worried people. I imagined it was the sort of party that World War One fighter pilots held.

As tables splintered and glass cracked Paula suddenly

kissed me on the cheek and said, 'Thanks, Kelvin, for doing all this.'

'That's all right,' I replied. 'It's what friends are for.'

'Is it, is that what they're for?' she asked, looking thoughtful. 'I'm not entirely sure. Loving people just seems to cause upset, you'd be better off without it.'

'Yeah, but you don't have a choice,' I said. 'See, I reckon each person's got their lifetime allocation of love, got a tipper truck's worth and they have to dump it somewhere. If you don't give your love to people you'll just end up forming strange attachments to garden furniture or peculiar political parties or yachting.'

She asked, 'How much cocaine did those two guys give you?'

I'd instructed Sidney to meet me at my place for our trip to Amsterdam. He arrived in a taxi, which surprised me because his wife usually drove him around during the day.

'Where's Barbara?' I asked.

'I think she's left me,' he said.

'Left you?'

'Well, no, she's just gone to Makro for the day with her sister so not left me but we're not getting on very well. I reckon it's only a matter of time.'

'Then it'll be nice for you to give her a break from you and you might return transformed.'

Showing him into my garage I said, 'I've got a present for you.' In the centre of the floor, propped upright, were two brand-new Silver Marin Alp bicycles, carbon forks, top-of-the-range Shimano twenty-one-speed gears, complete with rear rack and waterproof panniers.

'What's this?' he asked.

'Well, I thought what we'd do is we'd ride these bikes to Liverpool Airport, load them on the plane, then ride them into Amsterdam from Schipol and then we can use them to get around the town like all the Dutch do.'

'I can't ride no fooking bike to Liverpool Airport, it's like fifteen miles!' he shouted.

'It's only thirteen,' I said, 'and you'll enjoy it, mate, take your mind off things; exercise always improves a person's mood, gives you a rush of endorphins to your brain.'

'I don't want a rush of dolphins in my brain . . . can't do it, ain't ridden a bike for years.'

'It's just like riding a bike, you never forget.' Here I hardened my voice. 'Sidney, I've gone to a lot of trouble over this, mate; it would really upset me if we didn't do it.'

He paused; the calculations involved in pleasing a friend over pleasing just yourself were new to him. I could almost see the unused mental machinery clanking into life. When he spoke again the noises he made suggested a stalled apparatus uneasily grinding into renascence. 'Gnfft, I ahh mnngrn, I yahnn, I yahnn . . .'

'Look, I got these,' I said, holding up two in-helmet walkie-talkies. 'With these we can speak to each other as we ride along – won't that be cool?'

'Yeah, I suppose so,' he muttered.

'Great!' I said. 'Let's get going then.' And I began to transfer his belongings into the bike's panniers, adding, 'I bought you some special shoes to fit in the toe clips as well.'

For the first few miles I kept us to narrow back country lanes, a watery-eyed sun indifferently observing our efforts; cars here were few and those that passed swung out wide to give the wobbling, weaving Sidney as much room as possible. From time to time he pressed his 'Talk' button to try to speak to me but most of the time only a strained gasping would fill my helmet. I felt wonderful, this was easy for me; the susurration of the tyres on the road, the hedges and trees rolling past, the agreeable rhythm of my legs on the pedals, the sound of that bastard suffering behind me, all of it lulled me into a happy, reflective calm.

Once we had passed the point of no return I started to ease us on to busier and busier thoroughfares until, seemingly without warning, we were cycling along the East Lancashire Road, an extremely busy dual carriageway that leads to the northern edges of Liverpool. Every minute or so an articulated truck or an overloaded tipper would rocket past, the driver oblivious to the vulnerable little creatures grinding along in the gutter. The bellow of the truck's engines and the thunder of their many tyres tore at our ears, the vacuum dragging in their wake caused even me to have to fight with the bike's controls as these gigantic blocks of rushing metal exploded past us.

I heard Sidney's desperate panting in my ears. 'Christ!' he heaved. 'Those fucking trucks . . . I never knew . . . the size of them.'

'Yeah,' I replied, 'they're bastards, aren't they; they don't care whether you're there or not, they don't look.'

'Bastards . . .' he just about managed to hiss.

From the East Lancs I led him along the Queens Drive ring road heaving with smoky old Toyotas and dented Nissan vans. He was a game old sod, I had to give him that: though from time to time he would whine to me over the walkie-talkie about the pains in his legs, he kept going. From

Queens Drive in a brief faux rural idyll we cycled through Sefton Park, passing the aged silent trees, the huge sandstone mansions and the dead flowers tied by a dirty faded ribbon to a bough against which a young girl student had been crushed by joyriders five years before. Out of the park it was a straight eastwards run to Speke and Liverpool John Lennon Airport ('above us only sky').

A mile or so before the turning to the airport road we passed an area of factories and a low-rise warehouse shopping complex. For a while, apart from cars and trucks, we had been being overtaken by various rattling old buses that looked like they had been bought from Bombay City Council after they'd judged them unroadworthy. Red traffic lights forced us to stop at the junction of the access road to the shopping complex. I had briefly let Sidney go ahead as the lights turned to green and a grimy, rattling single-decker bus came churning alongside; without signalling it slowly began to turn left across our path into the trading estate, black smoke gouting from the slats of its ancient diesel engine. I heard Sidney yelling, 'No, hey no, hey, hey!' as the side of the bus began implacably driving him into the kerb, his bike being drawn inexorably under the wheels: it would have crushed him if he hadn't managed to wrench his feet from the toe clips and instead he was thrown in an arc through the air, to bounce down on to the rock-hard pavement.

The rear wheels of the bus passed over the bike, popping open the panniers and contorting its frame into tangled metal, then once round the corner it sped up in a cloud of black smog. I caught a glimpse of the driver gabbling away on his mobile phone as the bus disappeared from sight behind the corner of Allied Carpets.

As soon as I'd seen what was happening I had braked. Now I jumped my bike up on to the pavement and rode towards Sidney's unmoving body. Laying my Marin down on the ground and bending over his sprawled form I heard him groan, 'Oh, my fooking wrist.'

Uncertain whether I was relieved or not that he wasn't dead, I asked, 'Can you stand?'

He tried but gave a yelp of pain. 'No, I think my fookin' leg's broken as well.'

For the third time in my life I dialled the emergency services and was again connected with the same woman: I wondered if she recognised my voice as once more I requested that an ambulance be sent.

8

The Christmas shopping crowds surged this way and that, loaded down with carrier bags of straining plastic containing things they couldn't remember buying; I thought they could have all swopped shopping with each other and it wouldn't have made any difference. The *Big Issue* seller's dog had a Santa hat on and outside the Adelphi Hotel on Lime Street there was a man, some sort of Balkan refugee I guessed, wearing a flashing red nose and tinsel worn like a scarf round his neck, who stood tending to a battered metal cart from which a little later he was hoping to sell long sausages in doughy buns to drunk people.

The aroma of frying onions wafted over me and Florence as we climbed out of our chauffeur-driven Mercedes in front of the hotel. As I stood telling the driver what time to return to pick us up I saw the refugee look at Florence and Florence look back at the refugee, both of them scenting some sort of shared history. The aylum-seeking sausage seller was wearing a dirty grey sweatshirt with a big logo of Harvard University printed on it in black. Florence, noticing his shirt, said, 'Kelvin, I don't think that man been to Harvard University. Or if he did go der then that university certainly don't guarantee the good job it supposed to.'

I said, 'When I went to art school in London for that year our college scarf was a pickled conger eel.'

'Oh, har har, it's the funny man,' she said.

The penetrating scent of onions followed us through the revolving door and into the crowded foyer of the Adelphi, if anything making it smell a bit better than it had done moments before.

We eased a path through the drunken mob of revellers and the hotel's combative staff until we reached the entrance to the ballroom, inside which the annual dinner dance of the Merseyside Association of Builders and Developers was being held.

As we walked down the steps into the darker noise of the ballroom and picked our way between the many round tables, a number of fat builders started shouting remarks at us such as, 'Ready for inspection over here, Sergeant Major,' and 'Officer present! Hands off cocks grab your socks.' They called these things not at me, though I was very smart in my Hugo Boss dinner jacket but because of Florence, looking even more resplendent, wearing as she was the dress uniform of a major of horse in the regiment of the 14th Caucasian Mountain Lancers: her sabre in its scabard shimmying on the hip, black boots shining like molten tar beneath her knee-length dark blue skirt, the row of medals across her breast reflecting back light like anti-aircraft beams from the mirrorballs which hung over the dance floor and her cap pulled low over her eyes giving her a mysterious military veiled look. Her in that outfit excited me terribly; I felt like I'd found a whole new different level of sexual desire, as if I'd suddenly discovered my house had another entire floor I'd not been aware of before.

At the cost of a thousand pounds I had paid for a whole table for the night which seated eight people and entitled them all to dinner, dancing and self-congratulatory speeches by a succession of fat arses. When booking the table I'd informed Florence that the dinner dance was formal; almost my sole reason for doing it was because I really wanted to see her in an evening dress, a dress I wanted to pay for, a dress to show off her beautiful, taut body, to make all the other builders in Liverpool jealous of the quality of woman that was letting me fuck her.

'What is formal?' she asked.

'Well, you know, dinner jackets for the gentlemen, ball gowns for the ladies, that sort of thing.'

'I'm not wearing no fucking balls gown, I look like fucking pedigree pig.'

'You'll look lovely.'

'No . . . don't want.' She thought for a minute then said, 'Wait, at these things, do soldiers wear their dress uniform?'

'I guess,' I replied. 'I've only seen them do it in films but I guess you could.'

'Then I wear my old regimental dress uniform.'

'Your old regimental uniform?'

'Yes, see when I start to show promise as gymnast, back home when I was kid they make me squad leader in the young pioneers, get use of all the best facilities, then when I am sixteen I get commission in the army for same reason. They make me officer: Major of Horse in 14th Caucasian Mountain Lancers, the famous "Chimps"; that their nickname they got after the Battle of Lunjberg when they ran out of ammunition and pelted the Russians infantry with animals from the zoo.'

I'd already bought Florence her main Christmas present: a thing called a 'Disability Experience Suit'. This was a one-piece boiler suit-type garment into the lining of which had been sewn a series of jointed rods hinged where the wearer's limbs hinged; at each connection was a screw and bolt arrangement which could be tightened and stiffened, thereby giving the person dressed in the suit the experience of having a range of disabilities connected with rigidness and old age such as arthritis, rheumatism, osteoporosis and so on; at the screw's tightest setting, apparently, the salesman at Bell and Banyon had told me it was just like having motor neurone disease. There were in addition metal bands at the neck, wrists and ankles which could be tightened to cut off the blood supply to those limbs in order to feign multiple sclerosis. Also in this top-of-the-range model there were a number of pouches in the arms, legs and body into which could be slipped special bags filled with birdseed and lead shot to replicate what it was like for the wearer to be morbidly obese. I'd had the suit gift-wrapped and it was now waiting in my wardrobe like a beribboned and headless circus strongman.

As I said, I had looked on the dinner dance as the opportunity to show off Florence as well as a rare night away from Sidney Maxton-Brown. After the ambulance had taken him away from the site of the accident, I called my dad to come and pick up the wreck of Sidney's bike. He threw the tangled metal and wire into the back of his Volvo estate and though there was room in the passenger seat I cycled the mile and a half to his house. I made myself some cheese on toast in my father's spartan kitchen, then we watched a bit of horse racing on the TV, sitting side by side in his armchairs. After a while as the horses galloped round my dad asked, 'Son, anyone you fancy for the National next year?'

I replied, 'Well, they say Nicholas Hytner's production of *The Cherry Orchard*, should be the one to watch.' We did this joke every time we watched horse racing together so that we hardly noticed we were doing it. Nevertheless

I had always taken care to update my references over the years. I seemed to remember when we started doing it it had been Richard Eyre's production of *The Government Inspector* that I'd used.

'So he's a mate of yours is he, that Sidney bloke?' my father asked.

'Yeah, he's a mate . . . we go cycling together and that.'

'Funny-looking fella,' said my dad, 'knows an awful lot of swear words.'

'Well, he was in pain.'

'There's still no call for that kind of language.'

I left my bike in his shed and took a taxi the whole fourteen miles home. It was only after I paid the taxi driver off that I recalled he hadn't told me a terrible story: in fact now that I thought of it, no stranger had confided in me for weeks; the flood of awful reminiscences seemed to have stopped.

Sidney had no broken legs, simply a fractured wrist and torn ligaments in both knees. He spent a night in the Royal Liverpool Hospital, then his wife had come and driven him back to the farm. I let him stew for a few days before going to visit at his log house.

He lay propped up in bed, eyes staring out of the floor-to-ceiling glass windows at the bare trees and frozen ground along the edges of his land.

'How are you, mate?' I asked. 'Barbara says you're a bit low.'

'I do feel a bit low,' he replied, still not looking at me. 'I been crying a lot.'

'That's not like you,' I said, secretly thrilled.

'No, well, I been thinking about things . . .' Sidney paused. 'Kelvin, do you think you're a nice bloke?'

'Well, yeah, I guess so,' I replied.

Sidney went on, 'They say "even Hitler thought he was a nice bloke" but I wonder sometimes about me . . . these days, if I'm worth knowing. I used to think I was a great bloke, now I dunno so much. Honest, Kelvin, sometimes I think it's only having a mate like you keeps me sane.'

Along with Florence I'd decided I wanted to invite Paula and Adam to the dinner dance at the Adelphi as a way to celebrate the young man's release from Muddy Farm; the other four guests for the night were my two best employees and their wives, the men crammed into cheap dinner jackets, the women dressed in ball gowns that made them look like baroque Belgian cathedrals. My employees had been there since the doors opened; Paula and Adam arrived a little while after me and Florence.

Rapidly we were served the sort of Christmas dinner you might get in a reasonably well-run open prison. As Adam sipped at a mineral water and chatted to my site manager's wife about her whippets, Paula and I talked, for the first time sober, about the old days.

I said as my desiccated dinner was thrown down in front of me with a thump, 'Can you remember all the terrible pretentious restaurants we used to go to?'

'Not all of them,' she replied, 'who could? I do recollect the big Cajun cooking explosion of '92, remember that? We all went to a restaurant in Clitheroe called Mississippi Burning, and Colin said if he wanted his catfish blackened he'd move to a polluted part of the Ukraine, thank you very much.'

On my other side Florence said, 'You know when I first came to England and I see a sign saying "Pub Grub" I think that the pub have some kind of weevil that they were really proud of.'

'Having eaten in a lot of pubs I wouldn't be surprised if they had been serving weevil,' Paula said.

After the meal and the speeches the Kevin Stuart Eleven played for us; as it got later they were replaced by a DJ spinning the more melodic chart stuff. My beautiful girlfriend suddenly stood and said across the table, 'Hey, Adam, you want to dance with me?'

'Only if you take your sword off,' he retorted, though clearly delighted at the prospect.

'Sure,' she said, unbuckling the scabbard and throwing it down amongst the wine bottles and coffee cups. She then took off her cap, shaking her black hair loose and undid the top of her tunic down to a lacy bra that showed the round tops of her breasts. Taking the boy's hand she led him beaming on to the dance floor.

'So Adam's great now,' I said.

'Yeah, he seems fine,' Paula responded. 'And Florence, wow, what a girl! She's wonderful, you've got somebody very special there, Kelvin.'

'I know.'

As we watched her son dancing with Florence, Paula said, 'Hey, do you remember how people used to get ratty with us because we talked all the way through films and plays and stuff?'

'I know it used to upset Sage Pasquale tremendously but the rest of us felt we had such interesting things to say it would be a shame to keep them to ourselves, or worse still to hold them in till the interval by which time we might have forgotten them.'

There was a pause while we recalled our younger ghosts.

Then I said, 'You know, Paula, if I met us now I'm not sure I'd like us much, never mind that we would all become friends.'

'No, I guess we might have come across as kind of smug and annoying,' she said. 'We were drawn to each other at first then once somebody is your friend and they change in ways you don't like you sort of make excuses for them simply because they're your friend.'

'That's right!' I said. 'And now I just think maybe that I ended up with the wrong friends. You know when I . . . when they were alive I think as a person I was a sort of vacuum that they filled up. I got all my ideas from them, mentally checked my beliefs against what they would say even before I expressed them, even if they weren't around they were a little advisory panel in my head. Now, though, I feel that at last I'm me, my thoughts, my opinions come only from me. Even if Florence and Si . . . the other new friends I've made all disappeared, I don't think I'd change now. This is me now and this is how, in essence, I will remain.'

'What, you wouldn't miss Florence if she went?'

'Of course I would. Jesus, she's one of the main reasons I am the way I am, she's shown me how to be myself. When you look at her, she's suffered so much and yet it hasn't spoiled her, she's totally original. Yet if she went my belief is I would still be me, sad but me, there's nothing that can happen to me now that would change me.'

'Well that's great.'

Florence returned to our table, sweat plastering her hair down.

'Hi, where's Adam?' she said.

'We thought he was with you,' replied Paula, stiffening.

'No, he left me ten minutes ago. I've been dancing with some quantity surveyors.'

We searched all over the public rooms of the hotel for Adam but couldn't find him anywhere. We recognised at the start that it was pointless. Had known from the outset that he was outside somewhere, in the city looking for drugs, just as I'd known all along, but had chosen to bury the knowledge, that there had been something fake in his recovery.

You get a routine in these things quite quickly, who to call, where to look. Machsi phoned back two days later to let me know where Adam could be found: it wasn't a good place.

Telling his mother he was more or less safe, I said I supposed I'd go and fetch him. She told me to do whatever I wanted in a flat emotionless voice. Not understanding her tone, I would have talked to her further but suddenly an idea began to form in my mind. I quickly rang off then called Sidney.

'Sidney,' I said, 'I've got to go somewhere and I thought you might like to come with me.'

'I don't know, mate,' he replied, 'I'm not feeling too good.'

'A little run out, mate, 'll do you the world of good and there's somebody I want you to meet. I don't want to say too much but I've got a feeling this person can make you better.'

He perked up at this. 'You sure?' he asked, suddenly some faint eagerness entering his voice.

'I think there's a good chance,' I said. 'Look, I'll come and get you in the car.'

'Oh, I suppose so,' he grudgingly agreed, a few seconds' enthusiasm having tired him out.

* * *

I drove out to Sidney's farm and collected him. Never one to look after his appearance, he had for a while when feeling good made an effort at looking sharp; now he'd gone backwards, passing the state of greasy dishevelment he'd been in when I'd first met him. Today he was wearing saggy black tracksuit bottoms, dirty tartan slippers and a T-shirt that'd shrunk to expose a crescent of his distended belly; the T-shirt had printed on it: 'November 9th. British Sausage Week' and below that a big picture of a sausage. Pulling on a faded stonewashed denim jacket, he followed me out to the car.

Thirty minutes driving from Sidney's place, under a cold grey sky pendulous with snow, country roads gave way to an almost untravelled dual carriageway. In due time I turned off this: all the road signs had been burned down, but fortunately I knew my way to the New Town. This was a truly misbegotten place, built in the 1960s when 'New' seemed to have been another word for 'cheap', 'shoddy' and 'grim'. The town reminded me of those fake settlements I'd seen on the Discovery Channel constructed on army bases for the SAS to practise their house-to-house fighting in; any second I expected a cardboard terrorist to pop up in a glassless window. A narrow road carpeted with glass took us to a small estate of houses built on dead-end streets: breeze-block walls and a brick skin with no insulation between, guaranteeing greeny-black mould on the walls; cheap single-glazed steel windows dripping with condensation on the inside, and, behind the cracked, peeling white fascia board, there'd be a flat asphalted roof with no covering so in the summer it would heat up then cool down, creating fissures through which the winter rain was now leaking.

On the way Sidney, sunk into silence, suddenly enquired, 'So where we going?'

When I told him the name of the town he said, 'He's not some sort of therapist, is he? I'm not seeing no therapist and telling him my secrets.'

'No, not a therapist, no.'

On the dead-end estate street the only other car was a silver BMW 3 series convertible that was parked outside one particularly beat-up-looking house. We pulled up next to it. The driver, one of Machsi's, a little bantam in bomber jacket and baseball cap, got out. I had the feeling he'd been allowed to borrow the car for the afternoon.

'He's in 'ere,' he said, led us up the path of one house and hammered on the door. A huge black guy in a vest and satin boxer shorts opened it. 'These are the ones who've come for the kid,' then he added, 'all right?' with just enough threat in it to make the guy who opened the door back down from any objections he might have made. Turning to us, the little man said, 'You shouldn't 'ave no trouble,' and walked back to his car, started it up and drove away.

We entered the hall, the black guy closed the door behind us. He said, 'The lad's upstairs in one of our executive doubles.'

I snorted through my nose in acknowledgement of the joke but Sidney whined, 'I don't like this, what's going on?'

'Hey,' I said, grabbing his arm, 'do you want to be better or not?'

'Yes, I suppose . . .'

'Come on then.'

The hall still contained relics of the last normal ones to occupy the house: a wrought-iron telephone table and an orange plastic lampshade on the dead light fitting. Elsewhere there was nothing at all. Through the doorless doorways I could see inside the downstairs rooms stained mattresses spread around on the floor with bedspreads pinned across the windows to keep the light out. On each mattress lay a slumped form, each one looking more like clothes left outside a charity shop than a person.

Upstairs it was the same. In a back bedroom beneath a torn poster for N' Sync the custodian indicated one form, Adam; in the other corner a junkie, noting a change in the air pressure in the room, sat up and looking straight at me said, ''Scuse me, mate, I've run out of petrol and I need to get me daughter to her ballet lesson. Do you think you could lend me seventy-eight pence for a litre of unleaded?'

'No,' I said.

'Fair enough, please come again,' replied the junkie and collapsed back on to the mattress.

I turned to Sidney. 'This is him,' I said, indicating Adam.

'Eh?'

'This is him.'

'How can 'ee make me better?'

'Well,' I said, feeling dizzy anticipation, like I was about to step on to a frightening theme park ride, 'you know that accident you told me about that you had last year? The one where you killed those people?'

'Yeah, I've been a bit—'

I cut him off. 'This is the son of one of those you ran into. Before you killed his dad he was a fine boy, good student, nice lad. This is what you made him, a fucked-up junkie . . . you made him.'

'I didn't! I didn't!' he shouted. Then in a quieter voice, 'How's that going to make me feel better?'

'I didn't say feel better, you cunt, you don't deserve to feel better. I said "make you better" – a better person, better than the selfish, fucking murdering shite that you are now!'

'Why are you telling me this, why are you telling me this?' he pleaded, looking around for a way out. Then, after a perplexed pause, 'What's it got to do with you?'

'Because they were my friends that you killed,' I yelled, going right up to him, screaming into his face. 'It was me driving behind them, it was me saw you hit them! It was me saw you kill them. Why do you think I had so much time to hang around with a fat, shabby creep like you?'

'I thought you were my friend,' Sidney said in a sad little voice, staring down at the ground. 'I thought you were my friend.'

'No, I only pretended to be your friend to get you to see the fucking horror of what you done.'

'Oh, that's a very cold thing to do,' he said, then, struggling for breath, 'Well, congratulations.' Tears welled up in his eyes. 'I feel horrible now, are you happy?'

'Yes I am,' I stated, 'I certainly am,' though in truth I wasn't entirely sure what I was feeling. 'I'm very, very happy.'

Then we just stood there staring at each other. After a good two minutes had passed I finally said, 'Well?'

'Well what?' asked Sidney, looking bewildered.

'I dunno,' I said. 'I thought you might run off or something.'

'Why would I want to do that?' he enquired confusedly, spreading his arms wide. 'I'm stuck out here in bandit country in me slippers.' Then paused before adding, 'Anyway, I presume you need some help with the lad. You weren't planning to leave him here?'

'I guess so,' I answered, feeling vaguely discomfited like I'd somehow lost the initiative.

Slung between the two of us, Sidney and I hauled the comatose teenager down the narrow stairs and into my car.

The drive to Paula's house was spent in silence like a married couple who'd had a row. I parked outside, got out and knocked on her door. She answered it looking drained and ill.

'Hi,' I said, 'I've found him . . . Adam, I've got him in the car.'

She looked for a long time at her son slumped against the back window.

'I don't want him,' she said.

'What?'

'I don't want him,' she repeated. 'I've had enough, I can't take any more. He'll kill the two of us if we go on like this. He's going to have to sort himself out or to die. I don't know which; either way there'll be an end to it.'

'Well, what am I supposed to do with him?' I quavered.

'Leave him at a bus stop,' Paula said. 'I don't care. Just take him away from me.' With that she turned and slammed the door.

'She won't take him,' I said once back in the driving seat.

'She won't take him?'

'No.'

'What are you going to do then?' Sidney asked.

'She said I should leave him at a bus stop.'

'Which one?'

'I don't think she meant it literally.'

We sat in thoughtful silence until Sidney said, 'I'll take him then.'

'What?'

'I'll take him. You say I'm responsible for him being like this, so I'll take him.' With a strange sort of dignity he said, 'I'd like you to drive us to my house now, please.'

Again there was silence between us until we passed through the gates of his farm.

I got out and opened the back door so that Adam fell into my arms. Sidney came out the other side and helped me to get him upright. 'Right,' he said, 'let's put him in one of the ostrich sheds.'

'Aren't you going to have him in the house?'

'No, fuck off,' he replied. 'He's a fooking junkie. I'm not having him in the same house as me kiddies.'

So we dragged the boy, his trainers trailing through the wet grass, to a breeze-block shed with a corrugated plastic roof and a metal door. Inside, Sidney switched on a single harsh neon light to reveal a bare concrete floor and in one corner a pile of hessian sacking. 'Over there,' said Sidney, indicating the sacking. We dumped him down on to the mound then the older man squatted beside him and began to cover the boy with spare sacks. Without looking up at me he said, 'I'd like you to go now.'

'Er . . . right, okay,' I said, straightening. When I got to the door I turned back and saw that Sidney was still staring down at the recumbent teenager.

I didn't hear from him after that. I suppose I didn't expect to. I phoned Paula a few times to see if she knew anything: she told me she'd received a couple of picture postcards featuring views of Preston town centre on which her son had scrawled that he was okay and would be in touch at a later date, then there'd been nothing.

So much of my life had been devoted to those two that now I had a lot more free time. And I had to admit that I sort of missed Sidney, not in a good way or anything, or that I thought there was anything to like about him. I told myself I missed him more in the way that some recovering alcoholics miss their addiction in that they still have a vague sense that there's something they should be doing: that something being getting drunk, falling down in the gutter and vomiting blood on a trolley in casualty.

In January Florence packed her truck, said goodbye to the cirKuss and came to live with me. As we had pulled out of the cirKuss ground for the last time in Florence's behemoth I caught a glimpse of Valery standing where from my swaying passenger seat only I would see him. He made a strange gesture, one of those continental ones involving his arms, head, shoulders, three fingers and a thumb that seemed to convey an enormous number of things unsaid. This gesture expressed, as far as I could decipher it, loss, resignation, a certain wry amusement and mild seasickness, but I could have been wrong.

By then Florence had decided she didn't want to be an inventor but couldn't think of anything else; still, we had plenty of time. She drove her truck down to the local Ford dealers and was outraged when they wouldn't buy it for eight thousand pounds or swap it for a brand-new Ford Fiesta. In the end she donated the vehicle to a land-mine clearing charity based in Fleetwood and I bought her the Fiesta anyway.

As far as I could tell Florence didn't miss her old friends

or performing in the cirKuss at all. She seemed to be happy at my house without a job of any kind, watching daytime TV and going down to the shops or taking long walks in the countryside while wearing her Disability Experience Suit. Often she would get home from these trips after I did, returning with tales of how people had been kind or wicked to her that day, how she'd got stuck between the checkouts at Safeway's or a child had helped her on to a bus or how she'd fallen into the Leeds – Liverpool Canal and been rescued by some gypsies.

There was a 'French' restaurant in our little town that went by the name of Monsieur Le Frog. I liked it because it was a really old-fashioned, typically provincial place. English provincial, I mean, not French. The thing about successful restaurants in small places is that having nowhere else to go the clientèle keeps coming back week after week; for that reason they have to have very long menus or pretty soon the punters have eaten everything on offer. At Monsieur Le Frog the menu was a leather-bound document longer than the Treaty of Versailles. Over the years the two Egyptian owners had adapted to local tastes so amongst the classics like duck à l'orange, boeuf bourguignon and steaks with fifty-two different sauces, they also did a nice meat and potato pie with cabbage and parsnips. I was one of their regulars, which ensured that when I turned up one night with Florence there was a big welcome and we were seated in the nearest thing our small town had to a 'hot' table, the one they would have seated Robert de Niro at if he'd somehow taken a wrong turn off the M62.

While she seemed perfectly content watching TV and wandering the countryside dressed as an arthritic fat woman,

I considered that Florence was wasting herself. The woman was so talented, so beautiful, so extraordinary in her thinking, I thought it important that she expressed herself artistically. Congratulating myself that I wasn't the sort of man who selfishly wanted to keep his beautiful girlfriend at home like some delicate flower, I'd been thinking hard about what Florence could do next.

The waiter came and asked if we were ready to order; like the owners he was an Arab and in the days when my friends were alive I would have been unable to stop myself taking on a version of his accent, dropping in a couple of the odd words of Arabic that I knew, saying '*afwan*' and '*shukran*' while I requested my food; now I did none of that. I chose French onion soup with pesto ciabatta wedges followed by bacon ribs and a baked potato in my own voice, then said to Florence, 'Back in '95 me and my mates went on a clubbing weekend to Prague. There was a mental club scene there then, mostly run by the Ukrainian mafia, good drugs made by ex-East German sports scientists, naked girls in cage who'd do pretty much anything for ten dollars, excellent three-course meals for under two pounds. Anyway, this Czech girl I met told me that in the old Communist days the Communist Party that they had there running everything would decide what everybody should think about everything: pets, art, furniture. Apparently then they had these people called Political Commissars who would come down to work and tell you what you should think about pets, art, furniture. At the time it didn't sound that bad to me, to have somebody tell you what you thought all the time; it's a fucking pain sometimes having to think for yourself all the time.'

She said, 'Sure we had similar thing in my country but mind control isn't as much fun as you think; it was like everyone have to have two brains, "official thinking brain" for when in public and at school and so on and "private thinking brain" for when you with friends. It gets very confusing.'

Changing the subject I said to her, 'Florence, I was thinking, you remember when we did that play at the pub in the Crystal Quarter? *Christie in Love*? Well, I was thinking originally to have it just as a bar and restaurant but then I said to myself, what if there was a permanent performance space there with a nightly show, a cirKuss-type show, with you starring in it?'

'My own show?' she gasped, her eyes wide.

'That's right. You could either devise it yourself or get somebody else to do it and you could hire some other performers, other acts. I think it would make the restaurant really unique.'

'It might cost a lot of money,' she said, suddenly doubtful.

'Doesn't matter. I'll finance it, I seem to have the magic touch right now. I heard today from Laurence Djaboff that *Christie in Love* is going to open in London's West End at one of the big theatres.'

I could see the idea was taking root. 'My own show . . .' she mused. 'You know I have had an idea lately, while I was out walking, a story from my country about an eagle whose soul is stolen by a princess, then I think he becomes a train driver . . . anyway is great story. I could do it as a dance, acrobatic kind of thing.'

'Great, let's go and look at the space tomorrow.'

The next morning, early while it was still dark, my mobile phone rang: the caller ID showed it was Sidney's home calling; for a second I thought about not answering,

When I did it was Adam who spoke.

'Hi, Kelvin,' he said.

'Hello, Adam,' I replied cautiously. 'How you doing?'

'I'm good, Kelvin.'

'Great, I . . . we've been worried about you.'

'That's good of you.' Then he said, 'I'll get to the point. I was wondering if you could come out to Sidney's place, like maybe today if that's possible. There's something I'd like to say to you.'

I said, 'Yeah, sure, I can be there in a couple of hours.'

'Great, I'll see you there then.'

'Great.'

Telling Florence I'd meet her at the pub later that afternoon, I got into my car and gingerly steered it along the black-iced lane. The sun had arthritically edged its way into the sky and now shone bright on the frost-rimed fields as I drove along the familiar roads that led towards Sidney's farm. There was little other traffic: though it was late Febuary, increasingly it seemed people didn't get back from wherever they went for their Christmas holidays till round about mid March.

As I drove I tried to examine my feelings. As far as I could tell I realised that I was happy, all the last terrible vestiges of the fear that had followed me for so long had crumbled and blown away. I was healthy, prosperous and living with the most wonderful woman who was exciting, bold, beautiful.

I pictured what Adam had to say to me: supposing he wanted to thank me for what I'd done for him, all the money I'd spent, all the time I'd expended. I also thought that Sidney might be there and might want to say something similar. In my mind I rehearsed the gentle magnanimity with which I would accept their apologies.

After all, I had put a lot of effort into those two and if I was frank with myself, as I was trying to be, then I had to admit I sort of missed both of them. Of course it was Florence who meant the most to me, it was her love that had healed me, yet I wanted more – I wanted my cracked little family all back together again, Adam and Sidney and Florence.

The black gates swung back and I entered. Parking my car next to Sidney's Panther tank, a thin layer of dirty snow made it appear like a relic from the siege of Stalingrad. Feeling a little like Von Paulus, doomed commander of Sixth Army, I drew the lapels of my leather jacket up over my ears and walked towards the lair of my former enemy, my breath befogging the air.

The two of them came out on to the balcony as I approached and stared expressionless at me while I mounted the icy stairs. Adam looked thin, his hair cropped close to his skull; he was wearing a Gap T-shirt and jeans, clothes as blank as his countenance.

Sidney too had cut his hair short, making him look a lot younger and was dressed in fawn chinos and a light blue denim shirt.

'Hello, Kelvin,' Adam said.

Sidney grunted, 'Kelvin.'

'Guys,' I replied.

'Come inside,' the younger man said and led the way into the big living room. Sidney smiled quietly at the boy, seemingly unfazed by his proprietorial air.

I had rarely been in this room; like the rest of the house the walls and floor were pine with big glass windows looking out on to the pale winter countryside. The furniture was the big gloomy stuff middle-class Italians were fond of, dark brown wood tortured into a variety of swirls and curlicues, lots of marble and silk, gilt-framed paintings of non-existent forests. I sat down in an armchair, Sidney and Adam facing me on the couch. The teenager spoke.

'So . . .' He seemed both a lot younger and a lot older than his real age.

'Me and Sidney . . .' He paused then continued. 'We thought it was important to get you out here to speak to you and to tell you that we both forgive you . . .'

I went deaf for a minute, so that when I came to he seemed to be saying something about cricket and was forced to say, 'Whoa, whoa, back up a minute there. *You* forgive *me*?'

'That's right, we do.'

'The two of you?'

'Yes,' said Sidney, speaking for the first time since we'd sat down.

'What the fucking hell have you got to forgive me for?' I yelled, standing up. 'You, Adam, all I ever did was look after you and pay for you to go to treatment centres and worry about you.'

'That's what I've got to forgive you for,' the boy said, and it struck me right there and then what cruel little pricks young people could be. 'When you looked after me and sent me to Muddy Farm. I'm afraid my mum wasted your money there, Kelv.'

'Thanks,' I said, noticing he didn't mention anything about paying any of it back.

'See, you were delaying my recovery by doing all that. When you rescued me all the time, dusted me down and stood me up, you only enabled me to get back into taking drugs all over again. It was only Sidney who helped me to hit my rock bottom.'

'The point from which he could bounce back,' added the older man, in exactly the same tone of voice. It was like they had been taking Linguaphone lessons together in how to talk like a patronising cunt.

'He put you in an ostrich shed!' I shouted.

'Calm down, Kelvin,' Adam said in this incredibly annoying voice, 'and sit down.'

I had to force myself to control the rage I felt but did so.

'That's right,' he continued, 'Sidney did nothing for me thus allowing me to find my own recovery.'

'All right, okay, all right,' I said, my chest feeling tightly clamped so that my voice came out all taut and reedy. 'I can just about understand that I might have been doing the wrong thing for you – from the right motives I might add – but' – and here I pointed towards Sidney – 'I don't see what that cunt has got to forgive me for.'

'Maybe I should let Sidney answer that himself,' replied Adam, and I swear the two of them smirked at each other.

'Yes I will, Adam,' the older man said, then, turning to me, 'You see, Kelvin, first of all I have to tell you that Adam has explicitly told me he doesn't hold me at all responsible for what happened to his father; he's made it very clear to me that that was your shit, your shit that you were laying on me and him.'

'But you killed five people!'

'Did I, Kelvin?' he said. 'Or do you just think I did? I admit you had me convinced for a while. After all, you went to incredible lengths to make me think it was so and for a while I admit you made me feel extraordinarily bad. That's what I forgive you for. I hated you for a long time because you pretended to be my friend then you turned on me. I was devastated, but me and Adam have talked about it a lot and we now realise that you were taking out your guilt on us.'

'What fucking guilt?' I yelped. 'What fucking guilt?'

Sidney said, 'When a person comes through something that's killed others, then sometimes they feel bad that they didn't die too. Especially if their feelings for those people were . . . what's that word?'

'Ambiguous,' Adam chipped in. 'It's called survivor guilt, Kelvin,' said the boy.

'It's called horse shit,' I said, standing again. 'I've had enough of this. I'm going now.'

'Of course,' I heard Sidney saying, 'but we're not going to let you go, you know. You made me your friend and I'm going to continue that friendship. We'll call you in a couple of days.'

'I might not answer,' I said petulantly.

'I think you will,' Sidney responded with confidence; for the first time his two eyes seemed to agree – they both expressed a supercilious contempt for me.

'Goodbye, Kelv,' said Adam.

I walked out of that pine coffin of a house and got in my car.

I stood on a small hill I'd had built and surveyed it all. Phase One of the Crystal Quarter had been completed. The terraced houses around the forest were occupied, curtains and blinds in their windows, cars parked outside. There were a pair of skaters skittering loops on the frozen River Anfield and a man walked his dog on the cobbled path that meandered across the development. A small unthreatening sculpture was scheduled to be placed on the peak of the hill within a month.

Work on Phase Two, the new Victorian warehouses and the gym building, had begun, the foundations were dug and the concrete was due to be poured tomorrow.

My mobile phone rang – the site agent with a query. After I'd dealt with the call and rung off it suddenly occurred to me that another phenomenon that had ceased was the threatening messages from Valery. It had certainly been weeks now since he'd called. Perhaps because the intimidation seemed to have stopped I began to think about what he'd said in a different way; it struck me that even though I knew he was capable of it, he'd never taken any action. 'If he wasn't threatening me then what did he mean?'

Winter darkness seemed to come on as I walked across the site and squeezing past Florence's Fiesta entered the cold, empty pub: the bare plaster walls still exuded something of the wet clay smell of every building site but the kitchens were now in, the bar counter with its scrolled supports had been newly varnished and the electrics, water and gas would be connected in a couple of days.

She wasn't in the main space. I shouted, 'Florence! It's me!'

'Upstairs, sweetheart.' Her voice came from somewhere upstairs. Climbing the railless stairs took me to the second floor; up there we had retained the original room plan and the corridors were dark and unlit. A narrow staircase behind a propped-open tongue-and-groove door led upwards again into one of the four conical towers of the pub. She was there in the last of the twilight. Out of the curved windows were the lilac-grey ripples of North Wales and the flat aluminium expanse of the river estuary. Beyond the building site the orange balls of sodium light were glimmering on.

She stood by the window in the dissolving light. I felt I

had never loved her more than at that moment, the one solid thing in my life. Work had still not been quite completed up here; where she stood the floor was littered with planks of wood, strips of plastic and broken bricks.

Without looking at me she said, 'Darling, you have given me so much with the money to do my show that I think I have to give you something back.'

'No,' I said, 'you don't need to.'

'Yes, I will give you the whole of me now, it's time I finally told you my story. It's time that you know the things that happened to me, the reasons I left my homeland, time for all that.'

Feeling thrilled and apprehensive at the same time I thought, This'll make this awful day better. I can stand anything with Florence at my side to see me through it.

She turned from the window and looked at me for the first time. 'So,' she said, then returned to the view, except I felt she wasn't seeing Merseyside but rather the distant hills of her own land. 'One day some government soldiers came to our village. They told us that the Muslims in the next village had killed all the Christians like us the day before, so the men go and get their hunting guns and the soldiers give us some other guns and grenades, then we go and we get all the Muslims in our village and we put them all in their mosque and they all saying, please don't hurt us and we say, of course we don't hurt you, we know you since schooldays. Then we lock the doors and we set fire to the mosque and they start coming out of the windows and the men shoot them and throw in the grenades. I walk a bit away then I see down by the river a Muslim woman and her daughter I was at school with and they submerged so the tops of their heads only showing, so I go to our house and I get an axe then I go back to the river and I always hating her because they have a Volkswagen Golf that they swank about in and she see me and she stand up all wet and say please don't hurt me and please don't hurt my daughter but I hit them both with the axe over and over and over until they dead.

'Then a bit later the Christians come from the other village and they not dead after all but they say they will go back and kill their own Muslims now. Anyway now we killed all our Muslims and my husband go with them but some Muslims know they are coming maybe and ambush them on the path in the forest and my husband I think is killed. He don't come back anyway and then I think perhaps I have to leave.' She paused. 'It was a very very bad situation. I glad I told you everything now. Ah, this is so beautiful,' she said. 'I truly think I like to spend the rest of my life here.'

I imagined there might be a simple plastic switch in some dark basement and if you flipped this switch then everything in the world would stop. I knew that desire was not to be granted as sounds from outside were merging with the crackling in my head – a distant rumble of traffic, the barking of a dog. Well if the world was doomed to continue perhaps I would see to it that I never spoke again

I considered the idea that if I retreated towards the steep stairs that led to the turret I could throw myself backwards down them. In addition to my real injuries I could pretend to have brain damage that prevented me speaking; I would never talk again, shut up and not say another word ever. I'd indicate through hand signals and pencilled notes that I wasn't unhappy or anything, smiling and gesturing like a soft lad. Once a little time had passed Florence, my dad, my employees, they'd come to accept it; that would just be me – my thing, the one who didn't talk.

Unfortunately what you wish for doesn't always appear to come true so, remaining upright and upstairs, I said, 'Here, Florence, I heard this joke the other day. How do you kill a circus?'

'I don't know,' she replied absentmindedly, her thoughts all still on the view or her past or fuck knows what.

'Go for the juggler,' I said.

'I don't get it, funny man,' she replied.

I now stood at Florence's back. There was a big deep hole over the way scheduled to be filled with concrete first thing tomorrow morning that she would fit in nicely. I looked at her white neck, stretched my shaking hands out towards it then stopped; instead, from behind I put my arms around her waist and kissed the back of her head, burying my face deep in her black, black hair. The pies, the pies, I thought, the pies, the pies.